LAURIE COLWIN

HAPPY ALL THE TIME

PUBLISHED BY POCKET BOOKS NEW YORK

Portions of this book have appeared in *Cosmopolitan* and in slightly different form in *Redbook* under the titles of "The Girl with the Harlequin Glasses" and "Late Romantic" and in a volume published by Viking Penguin, Inc. entitled *Passion and Affect* under the titles "The Girl with the Harlequin Glasses" and "Passion and Affect."

Grateful acknowledgment is made to the following for permission to reprint previously published material: Doubleday & Company, Inc.: Four lines from "Le Lai de L'Ombre" in *Lays of Country Love* by Patricia Terry. Copyright © 1963 by Patricia Terry. Used by permission of Doubleday & Company, Inc.

POCKET BOOKS, a Simon & Schuster division of
GULF & WESTERN CORPORATION
1230 Avenue of the Americas, New York, N.Y. 10020

Published by arrangement with Alfred A. Knopf, Inc.,
a division of Random House, Inc.
Library of Congress Catalog Card Number: 78-2425

ISBN: 0-671-82777-4

First Pocket Books printing September, 1979

10 9 8 7 6 5 4 3 2 1

Trademarks registered in the United States and other countries.

Printed in the U.S.A.

For Ann Arensberg

PART ONE

CHAPTER 1

GUIDO MORRIS AND VINCENT CARDWORTHY were third cousins. No one remembered which Morris had married which Cardworthy, and no one cared except at large family gatherings when this topic was introduced and subjected to the benign opinions of all. Vincent and Guido had been friends since babyhood. They had been strolled together in the same pram and as boys were often brought together, either at the Cardworthy house in Petrie, Connecticut, or at the Morris's in Boston to play marbles, climb trees, and set off cherry bombs in trash cans and mailboxes. As teenagers, they drank beer in hiding and practiced smoking Guido's father's cigars, which did not make them sick, but happy. As adults, they both loved a good cigar.

At college they fooled around, spent money, and wondered what would become of them when they grew up. Guido intended to write poetry in heroic couplets and Vincent thought he might eventually win the Nobel Prize for physics.

In their late twenties they found themselves together again in Cambridge. Guido had gone to law school, had put in several years at a Wall Street law firm, and had discovered that his heart was not in his work, and so he had come back to graduate school to study Romance languages and literature. He was old for a graduate student, but he had decided to give himself a few years of useless pleasure before the true responsibilities of adulthood set upon him. Eventually, Guido was to go to New York and take over the stewardship of the Morris family trust—the Magna Charta Foundation, which gave money to civic art projects, artists of all sorts, and groups who wished to preserve landmarks and beautify their cities. The trust put out a bimonthly magazine devoted to the arts called *Runnymeade*. The money for all this came from a small fortune in textiles made in the early nineteenth century by a former sea captain by the name of Robert Morris. On one of his journeys, Robert Morris had married an Italian wife. Thereafter, all Morrises had Italianate names. Guido's grandfather was Almanso. His father was Sandro. His Uncle Giancarlo was the present administrator of the trust but he was getting on and Guido had been chosen to be eventual heir.

Vincent had gone off to the University of London and had come back to the Massachusetts Institute of Technology. He had begun as a city planner, but his true field of interest was sanitation engineering, as it was called, although Vincent called it garbage. He was fascinated by its production, removal, and possible uses. His monographs on recycling, published in a magazine called *City Limits,* were beginning to make him famous in his field. He had also patented a small machine for home use that turned vegetable peelings, newspapers, and other kitchen leavings into valuable

9

mulch, but nothing much had happened to it. Eventually he would go off to New York and give over his talent and energy to the Board of City Planning.

With their futures somewhat assured, they lolled around Cambridge and wondered whom they would marry.

One Sunday afternoon in January, Vincent and Guido found themselves perusing an exhibition of Greek vases at the Fogg Museum. The air outside was heavy and wet. Inside, it was overheated. It was the sort of day that forced you out of the house and gave you nothing back in return. They had been restless indoors, edgy out of doors, and had settled on the Fogg feeling that the sight of Greek vases might cool them out. They took several turns around. Guido delivered himself of a lecture on shape and form. Vincent gave his two minutes on the planning of the Greek city-state. None of this quieted them. They were looking for action, unsure of what kind and unwilling to seek it out. Vincent believed that the childish desire to kick tires and smash bottles against walls was never lost but relegated, in adulthood, to the subconscious where it jumped around creating just the sort of tension he was feeling. A sweaty round of handball or a couple of well-set cherry bombs would have done them both a lot of good, but it was too cold for the one and they were too refined for the other. Thus they were left with their own nerves.

On the way out, Guido saw a girl sitting on a bench. She was slender, fine-boned, and her hair was the blackest, sleekest hair Guido had ever seen. It was worn the way Japanese children wear theirs, only longer. Her face seemed to print itself on his heart indelibly.

He stopped to stare at her and when she finally looked back, she glared through him. Guido nudged

Vincent and they moved toward the bench on which she sat.

"The perspective is perfect," said Guido. "Notice the subtlety of line and the intensity of color."

"Very painterly," said Vincent. "What is it?"

"I'll have to look it up," said Guido. "It appears to be an inspired mix of schools. Notice that the nose tilts—a very slight distortion giving the illusion of perfect clarity." He pointed to her collar. "Note the exquisite folds around the neck and the drapery of the rest of the figure."

During this recitation, the girl sat perfectly still. Then, with deliberation, she lit a cigarette.

"Notice the arc of the arm," Guido continued. The girl opened her perfect mouth.

"Notice the feeblemindedness that passes for wit among aging graduate students," she said. Then she got up and left.

The next time Guido saw her, she was getting on the bus. The weather had become savagely cold and she was struggling to get change out of her wallet but her gloves were getting in her way. Finally, she pulled off one of her gloves with her teeth. Guido watched, entranced. She wore a fur hat and two scarves. As she came down the aisle, Guido hid behind his book and stared at her all the way to Harvard Square, which was, it turned out, their common destination. They confronted each other at the newsstand. She looked him up and down and walked away.

Two weeks later she turned up under more felicitous circumstances. She appeared at a tearoom with a girl named Paula Pierce-Williams, whom Guido had known all his life. Paula waved at him, and he ambled over to their table.

"Guido, this is Holly Sturgis," said Paula. "And Holly, this is Guido Morris."

"We've met," said Holly Sturgis.

"I never see you anymore, Guido," said Paula. "Are you still working on your thesis?"

"I'm almost finished," said Guido.

"I can never remember what it's on," said Paula.

"Medieval property law and its relationship to courtly love," said Guido. Holly Sturgis snickered.

Guido was not in the habit of falling in love with girls he saw on buses or in museums. He had had two serious love affairs and a small number of casual encounters. These he tried not to think about—they had puzzled and hurt him. He explained to himself that he was an old-fashioned man living in modern times, shackled with the belief that all real love affairs led to marriage. If they did not, they must in some way be bogus, built on bad faith or lack of true emotion. Therefore they were bad—once they were over, no matter how ardently one had begun them. The casual encounters Guido chalked up to sheer impulse. You could not call something that lasted for a day a love affair. Vincent tried to explain that these things were a matter of process—the process of growing up, but this was no consolation to Guido. In the case of his two serious love affairs, the partings had been equitable but not understandable: both the girls had married and sent him cards at Christmastime. Where, he wondered, had all that feeling gone?

Now as he entered his thirties, he believed that one made mistakes in love until one was perfectly sure. That surety found its object in Holly Sturgis. He was serious in matters of the heart, and serious in matters of aesthetics. Something about Holly Sturgis struck him profoundly. One look announced her elegance and precision. Everything about her—the calculation of her moves, the grace with which she walked, the fact that she took off her gloves with her teeth—moved him. He believed that desire was mere shorthand for aesthetics and intuition. He wanted Holly Sturgis, plain and simple. He wanted access to that sleek, vital Japanese hair. He wanted her naked in his naked arms. He imagined that her shoulders smelled coolly of jasmine.

In the way of people who fantasize rather than analyze, he knew that Holly was probably difficult, quirky, and hard to live with. It was obvious that she was precise—even her hair was precise. He knew all this because his daydreams were usually accurate —Vincent said he was a visual thinker. And so he imagined himself and Holly lying against crisp white sheets at the Ritz-Carlton Hotel. He did not bother to imagine how they got there or what led up to it. There would be anemones on the night table. Holly's hair would look like a sable paintbrush against the pillow and in his daydream she was smoking, balancing the ashtray on her stomach. The late afternoon light would be fuzzy with smoke. She would be entirely silent. He, of course, would be consumed by the event—it would be the first time they had been to bed together—and he saw himself looking cautiously at Holly, but unable to tell what that lovely, intelligent face was expressing or concealing from view.

Paula Pierce-Williams poured the tea. Then she went off to make a telephone call.

"Did you engineer this?" Holly said.

"Certainly not," said Guido. "I can't help it if you follow me around."

"I don't find that amusing. What do you want?"

"I want you to be more gracious to people who fall at your feet."

"I don't notice you falling at my feet."

"Maybe you don't know how to look," said Guido. He saw Paula walking toward them and quickly

13

asked Holly to have dinner with him. To his astonishment, she said yes.

Their first encounter did not take place at the Ritz-Carlton, but at Holly's. The anemones Guido had daydreamed about were a series of ferns that hung above her bed and got into his eyes when he sat up. The sheets were crisp, but not white. They were printed with violets. The pillowcases were decorated with blue roses. Holly was smoking and the ashtray balanced on her stomach was a little Wedgwood plate decorated with black vines.

Holly's apartment was white and airy and it was as precise as Guido had imagined. Holly made small, absolute arrangements of things. On a white table was a bird's nest, an Egyptian figure in blue stone, a Russian match box, and a silver ink-well. The bed, before they had rumpled it, was made so that you could roll a dime across it. The sheets and pillows smelled of lavender.

It was better than a daydream, better than those highly ornate night dreams that leave behind a sweet taste of inexplicable happiness in the morning. Guido turned to Holly and touched her dark, shining hair. She was wearing coral earrings the size of tuxedo studs and nothing else. It was a cold, rainy Saturday afternoon in late March, and Guido felt quite wiped out by sensation. Everything seemed uncommonly rich to him: the print on the sheets, the pattern on the quilt, Holly's gleaming hair and earrings. Her shoulders did smell of jasmine. When Guido turned to look at her, he saw on her face the look he had known he would see—a look so private and impenetrable and unclear that it rendered anything he thought of to say inappropriate.

Holly was the granddaughter of old Walker Sturgis,

who had taught classics. Her father was an executive in a copper company and her mother wrote historical novels for children. She was an only child, an only grandchild, and she was nearly perfect. She had her own ways, Holly did. She decanted everything into glass and on her long kitchen shelves were row upon row of jars containing soap, pencils, cookies, salt, tea, paper clips, and dried beans. She could tell if one of her arrangements was off by so much as a sixteenth of an inch and she corrected it. She was constantly fighting off the urge to straighten paintings in other people's houses. In her own house, her collection of botanical watercolors was absolutely straight. The shoes in her closet were stuffed with pink tissue paper and her drawers were filled with lavender sachet. In each corner of her closet hung a pomander ball.

She liked to have tea on a tray and she was fond of unmatched china. The tray she brought to Guido held cups that bore forget-me-nots, a lily-of-the-valley sugar dish, a cream pitcher with red poppies, and a teapot covered with red roses and cornflowers. This tray, when set on the bed, contributed to Guido's sensory overload. He was touched to think that this effort had been made on his behalf, but when he got to know Holly better he learned that she made up identical trays for herself when she studied.

Guido had wondered if she knew how to cook. Her slight air of otherworldliness suggested that she did not, while her precision indicated that she did—in the way the Japanese did. He expected a dinner that looked like a painting. It turned out that she was a real marvel. Guido was surprised by the sheer deliciousness of it: food that good must, he felt, spring from a truly charitable, loving spirit. But charity did not seem to be in Holly's immediate emotional vocabulary. After a spectacular afternoon in bed, they

15

had spent the rest of the day in polite half silence. Therefore, dinner almost did him in. Not only did it taste wonderful, it looked wonderful. Guido pegged Holly as a strong domestic sensualist. She had a positive genius for comfort but he was only a visitor: that comfort had been created long before he met her.

He spent a sleepless night next to her, very much aware, even when he dozed, that he was sleeping in a stranger's bed. He dreamed brief, disconnected dreams and woke suddenly, unsure of where he was. The sight of Holly did not immediately locate him— she seemed so dreamlike and unapproachable. He spent a long time gazing at her and realized that he did not want to go to sleep. He did not want to miss a minute of her.

But he did sleep, and when he woke, she was nestled beside him. But would she nestle up so sweetly when awake? She woke with a little shrug and rolled away. Guido sat up, catching his hair in the hanging fern. He was very bleary and beset by impulses: he felt all awash. He wanted to turn Holly into water and drink her. He wanted to throw himself at her feet. He wanted to throw himself at her entirely. Holly turned over and looked at him.

"Say," she said. "Would you mind getting the papers?"

And so, Sunday morning, the occasion of their first breakfast together, found Guido walking through a light rain to get the papers. On the way back, he felt a slight foreboding: had her request been the intimate summons of a lover, or did she just want him out of the house? Or did she ask all her lovers to get the papers? Suppose she forgot all about him while he was gone and did not let him back in?

It had taken him an arduous two months to get

into Holly's arms—two months of dinners, walks, conversation, afternoons at museums, and long talks at night. He had never concealed his intentions. He did not say he was in love, but he did say that he was in pursuit. Holly said she would consider his pursuit. Other than that, she was unswervable, unflappable, untouched, and completely separate. She continued to see him, and Guido was left wondering what sort of test he was being put through, and whether or not he would pass.

One night, when he had been positively addled by desire, she went to her writing desk and with a gold pen wrote out a list that she then presented to him. It was, she said, a list of the things she liked about him. The list read: eyes, hands, shoulders, clothes, and height. Guido pressed for further information.

"I hate soft hands," said Holly. "Yours are nice and strong. Where did you get your calluses from?"

"Building bookshelves and fishing," said Guido. "Go on."

"Well, I admire your height and I like the way you carry yourself. I have always had a fondness for hazel eyes and whoever cuts your hair has struck the perfect balance between shagginess and propriety. I like dark-haired men. And I like the way you wear your clothes."

Guido was so unnerved by this recitation that he had to fight the impulse to run to a mirror to see if he were the man she was describing. Did he have hazel eyes? Was he tall? Did he have dark hair and was that hair midway between shagginess and propriety?

Now as he turned the corner to her flat, newspapers under his arm, he wondered at what point Holly had decided in his favor. She had arranged to spend Saturday afternoon with him and it was perfectly clear in what manner it was to be spent. But what did that mean? She treated him exactly as she had before, except now they were lovers, and now he looked like any of the sleepy, overcoated husbands walking home with the Sunday papers. He was struck with envy at the sight of them. He imagined them going home to secure marriages, well-cherished spouses who would greet them with warm kisses and a plate of eggs, or who would still be sleeping—warm, cozy, and comfortable—their romantic battles far behind them. It did not occur to Guido that some of these men might be single or divorced, or in a state of romantic torture exactly like his own. That imagined security pained Guido, who was not walking toward a safe haven but to an encounter with a stranger in a stranger's house.

Every morning Holly woke at eight. This morning had been no exception. Guido appeared with the papers at eight-thirty, lured Holly back to bed, and felt himself temporarily the king of the universe. Three hours later they were finishing breakfast and reading the paper, but the news had little charm for Guido. What appeared to him as a great event in no way altered Holly's routine. Every Sunday she read the paper in a certain order. This Sunday was no exception. She read the society pages first to see who was getting engaged or had gotten married. Then she read the obituaries to see who had died. She read the arts and leisure section with special attention to the garden page, although she had no garden. She read at least two articles in the magazine section, studied the recipe of the week with a frown of disapproval, and then breezed through the fashion pages to see if there was anything she approved of. While Guido was undergoing a fit of desire, she read a long article about morality and genetics and then concentrated with complete absorption on an essay outlining the pitfalls and benefits of teaching infants how to swim. It was clear that she did not want to be spoken to. She sat upright in her straight-backed chair, neat as a cupcake, wearing a linen night shirt. Watching her, Guido began to realize why most violent crimes take place in the home: he wanted to strangle her. He wanted to get his hands on her and make her his. Finally, she had read the paper. The dishes had been washed and Holly was about to begin the crossword puzzle when Guido grabbed her.

"Goddamn it, Holly. Doesn't any of this mean anything to you?"

"Any of what?"

"We just spent our first night together and here you are doing the goddamned puzzle."

"I do the puzzle every Sunday," said Holly. "And I was assuming that this was the first of many nights. Besides, I find all this too nerve-racking and so I like to put things into the most normal context. I don't want one of those strung-out love affairs that makes you lose weight and feel awful all the time."

There was nothing Guido could say to this. The first of many nights, she said. That phrase, in her cool, measured voice, undid him. And she was right to want everything normal. That sentiment moved him profoundly, as did everything else about her. For Guido was having one of those strung-out love affairs that made him lose weight and feel awful all the time.

But she did put the crossword puzzle down, and locked her arms around Guido's neck. It was clear she knew how tender and fragile men are in these matters.

It was late in the afternoon when they again climbed out of bed. Guido felt that time had frozen into one solid block and he was losing his bearings. He felt

19

swarmed by detail: her look, her hair, her body, those sheets, that French toast, the memory of that formal tea tray and naked Holly pouring tea into his flowered cup. He badly needed a change of context. He needed to get Holly on his turf, if only for a little while. He wanted to see Holly feel strange in his apartment in order to right the balance. The sight of Holly sitting in his chair would put the cap on the reality of her, once and for all.

She took his arm as they walked and when it began to drizzle she nestled closer to him under the umbrella. She was talking about men's apartments.

"I've seen a few," she said. "All you boys wear pressed shirts and have your shoes polished and behave like perfect gentlemen at the dinner table, but there's hair all over the soap and none of the dishes are properly washed. Or, on the other hand, you look like wrecks and your apartments look like monks' cells or a picture out of *Boy's Life* with the bed made with camp blankets and the fishing rods stacked neatly in the corner. Then, of course, there's the hunting print set. Big pictures of dead elks and club chairs and those footstools that have feet made out of tusks. Disgusting. I have never been in one of those apartments that didn't have wedding invitations with ducal crests on the mantel."

Guido's rooms were neat and orderly. There were no hunting prints and no tusks, and no wedding invitations with ducal crests. She admired his two framed drawings and the bronze panther that had been his grandfather's paperweight. She ran her fingers over his walnut cigar box. Then she took off her coat and did something that made Guido's heart turn over. She went through the kitchen cabinets, the icebox, picked glasses off the shelves and held them up to the light. In the bathroom she flipped back the shower curtain to inspect the hem and looked over the soap, to see if it had hair on it.

"Do you mind me doing this?" she asked. Guido was speechless. It was the most open-ended gesture he had ever seen. He had no idea what was meant by it. Was she checking him out? Curious about his arrangements? Malicious? Solicitous? Making sure they were made for each other? Was this a joke, or was she establishing a rapport with his apartment?

Suddenly, she turned on him.

"Either you have a girlfriend, a cleaning woman, or you are entirely compulsive," she said.

"I'm very orderly," Guido said. "Once in a while I get a kid in from the student agency to do some heavy cleaning. You'd be amazed how efficient budding sociologists and historians can be."

Holly sat down, as if at home. But, Guido wondered, would she be happy where there were no trays?

They went out for dinner and she spent the night. Her clothes hung neatly over the back of his chair. Guido would have gladly slept with her clothes too. He wanted every bit of her that he could get. He had never wanted anything so ardently in his life. In the middle of the night, he woke to ponder his feeling of deprivation, even though his heart's desire was closer than arm's reach. Now it was his—or was it? Holly slept effortlessly. She had made up her mind about him, one way or the other, but she kept her decisions to herself. Any fool would think that her complacency at the breakfast table, her inspection of his apartment, the deliberateness with which she opened her arms to him indicated that she had chosen him, but Guido was not any fool. He had had time to survey his cool, unflappable beloved. She withdrew as if withdrawal was as natural as drinking coffee, and she did not make emotional statements. Was this withdrawal or concealment, or had everything been settled to her sat-

21

isfaction? This stance of hers drove Guido into a lather of confusion, although he knew that everyone feels odd at the beginning of a love affair.

Guido was not a fan of rashness. He had only shown what he felt, not told. He had always known that once his affections were firmly placed, excess would rapidly follow. Now what he felt was the emotional equivalent of extreme thirst. He wanted to stay up all night and watch Holly, who had gone off to sleep and left him.

Vincent Cardworthy was the most open-minded, tolerant, intelligent, and cheerful person Guido had ever met. Although in matters of his own heart he was deeply muddled, Vincent was right on the money when it came to the affairs of others. Thus Guido took guidance from a man who constantly fell in— never fell in love—with vague blond girls who either were on the verge of engagement or had just left their husbands, or were recovering from some grand passion or were just about to leave on an extended tour of Europe, or were in fact European and just about to return to their native land. Guido thought these girls were far beneath Vincent, but Vincent did not appear to care, at least after the event. He began these affairs with high spirits and then rapidly became bored, but he never broke them off. He was either far too kind or far too removed to do so. Rather, he let life take over. Since none of these encounters was destined for success, they simply evaporated. Vincent was never unkind or cruel. He made appalling choices and then treated them very well. The sort of girl he liked was raw-boned and healthy. He liked a girl who always looked as if she had just left the tennis court or come in from a nice, long hike.

He liked girls from Vermont who had outgrown their horses and now owned hand looms and candle molds. He liked sleepy girls from Philadelphia with big teeth who bred water spaniels and were interested in local Republican politics. He liked rugged girls from the Berkshires who played touch football. Guido called this tendency "the coach's daughter syndrome" although Vincent had never known the daughter of a coach. He never went looking for these girls. Rather, he fell on them in the course of his life. That they all seemed to be the same girl Guido took to be a dire sign, but Vincent claimed he was cutting his emotional teeth, and that if these girls seemed unsuited to him, it was because he was extremely busy and had no time to find anyone suitable, which he took to be the sort of search one associates with the Holy Grail. He said he did not mind a lightweight. Guido said if any of Vincent's girls had been more lightweight, they would have floated away like dandelions in late July. But Vincent felt, as did Guido, that one is always foolish until one is correct. Around the time that Guido met Holly, Vincent seemed to be somewhat unhappy about his love life, but that didn't bother him overly much.

Vincent simply wasn't anxious. His idea of the life of the mind was exterior. It had to do with planning, statistics, computers, and studies. Guido, on the other hand, was a slave of the interior. He found Vincent's take on things refreshing.

One evening, when Holly went off to a concert with her grandmother, Vincent spent the evening listening to Guido.

"I want to marry Holly," Guido said.

"Last week you said she was hard to get through to," said Vincent.

"I don't care," said Guido. "No one is problem free."

"You certainly do look wonderful together. But you say she's unnecessarily complicated."

"She is, but I don't care."

"You seem to be saying 'I don't care' an awful lot."

"I don't care," said Guido. "I have never been so sure of anything in my life. It doesn't matter what she's like."

"Freud says that in big issues, like who to marry, it's only a question of what you feel."

"Where does Freud say that?"

"I don't know," said Vincent. "Daphne Meranty quoted it to me."

"Which one is Daphne?"

"She's the one from Bangor. Her father is a minister. He's very interested in Freud. He makes all his children read Freud and he makes his congregation read him too."

"Is she the one with the Airedales?"

"That was Ellie Withers, and it was wire-haired terriers."

"You're not going to marry Daphne Meranty, are you?" Guido said.

"Oh, no," said Vincent. "She's engaged. I was her last fling. That's how the subject came up, you see. Well, good luck. With Holly, I mean."

"Is that all you have to say?" Guido said.

"Well, if you say that you're more certain of this than anything else in your life, what else is there to say?"

Guido sat gazing at his best friend and third cousin. There was the slightest resemblance between them—in the way their thick hair fell and a little around the cheekbones. Vincent was ruddy and freckled. In sunlight, his hair was reddish. His light eyes were flecked with green. His clothes could never stay entirely on his body. He hated cuffs and so his sleeves were always rolled up. His long torso caused his shirttail to untuck. When one button of his shirt unbuttoned, two generally followed. Where Guido was elegant, lithe, and sensual, Vincent was casual, springy, and game.

Guido found it curious that Vincent—who spent his life as a scientist analyzing—simply lived, while Guido, who simply lived, spent his life analyzing. Vincent was sitting in front of his fake fireplace, tying flies under a high-intensity lamp.

"Well, say something," said Guido.

"Oh, for God's sake," said Vincent. "If you think it would be fun to marry Holly, marry her. I know it's all very serious but one of us ought to get serious. I guess I'll be the best man and have to throw you a party or something, huh? Your problem is you think too much. You agonize over everything. I never think about myself at all, which is clearly the better way. And now you have an issue that can't be thought about. Just marry her. Have you asked her?"

"No," said Guido.

"Well, get cracking, for God's sake. How can I be your best man if you haven't proposed? Your problem, Guido, is that you are a man of thought, not a man of action. Go ask her. I'm sure she'll say yes. Why haven't you, for God's sake?"

"Terror," said Guido.

A week later, Guido sat in Holly's living room watching her stand on tiptoe to water her plants. She watered them twice a week—the same days every week. She disappeared into the bedroom with her watering can. Guido held her image with him: her swanlike neck, that wedge of dark hair, the arch of her feet as she balanced on tiptoe.

"Guido," she called. "Come here."

He stood at the bedroom door.

"There's a little blue box in the squirrel-foot fern. Did you put it there?"

"Yes," said Guido.

"Why did you?"

"As a romantic gesture," Guido said.

"Is it a ring?"

"Yes," said Guido.

"I see," said Holly. "In that case, I think we ought to have a talk." Guido's heart lurched. This lurch was followed by a searing pain. There could be only one thing to talk about—she was going to turn him down. The fact that she was clutching the box did not console him.

"I'm going away for a week," said Holly. "I have to have a little uncluttered time to think in. I'm very introspective as a rule, but now I feel carried away. I can't think in context. I mean, I can't think about us while you and I are together. Do you see what I mean?"

"I don't," said Guido.

"What I mean is, this is all very serious. I mean, if I am going to marry you, I feel I ought to turn it around in my mind and if we're together, I get confused."

"I haven't asked you to marry me," said Guido.

"Then why have you stuck a ring box in my squirrel-foot fern?"

"As a romantic gesture." Guido sat down next to her on the bed. "Open it."

Inside the blue box was a mound of dark blue velvet, lying on top of which was a heavy yellow-gold ring with a flat turquoise in the center.

"I know you hate stones," Guido said. "And I know you hate any gold that isn't yellow. And I know you like weight." He knew more things: that she hated sheets that weren't pressed; that she thought suntans were show-offy unless gotten in the line of work; that she felt letters ought to be written with a fountain pen; that she took a stand against ice in drinks; that she took an equally firm stand against bright colors with the exception of red; and that she would eat oranges but nothing that was orange-flavored. He was deeply in love with these quirks and he felt that he could see the big picture beneath them. Guido believed in the meaning and integrity of gestures. Holly's habits, her rituals, her opinions stood for the way she felt about the world—they expressed some grand conception of life and the placement of things in it. Her perfection and precision were a noble stand against sloppiness. Nevertheless, these things were just about all he knew. She had never told him anything. Now he understood that she intended to marry him, but she sat on the bed with the ring in her palm and said nothing at all.

"Do you like it?" Guido said.

"It's perfect," said Holly. "I love it." He could not see her face. Her head was bent and all he could see was her glossy, sable hair.

It fit, of course, perfectly.

"I do want to marry you," said Guido. "I mean, I want you to marry me."

Holly looked up at him with a look of slight surprise. Wasn't it a done thing? she seemed to say.

"It's only a question of when," Holly said. "But I want to go away first. I want to feel what it's like to be without you so I can know what it's like to be with you. Does that make any sense?"

"No," said Guido.

"Well, what I mean is, I'm used to our connection and I'd like to disconnect just to feel the power of that connection. You can't feel that unless you reconnect and you can't reconnect without disconnecting. Stop looking at me like that, Guido."

"I was only beginning to realize that I am about to marry someone who doesn't make a shred of sense."

"I do make sense," Holly said. "I just can't see things up close. Then I get intrigued by the idea of distance."

A tiny shiver went through Guido. That sounded like a phrase he would one day remember.

"Holly?"

"Yes?"

"I have no idea how you feel about me."

"Don't be silly. Of course you do. I'm going to marry you, aren't I? It's just a week apart."

During that week, Guido made a stab at pretending he had never met her. He went to the library. He wrote the final chapter of his dissertation. He went to a basketball game with Vincent and then went out and drank too much beer. Vincent refused to discuss Holly with him, so they talked about Vincent's mulch machine, the stock market, and where they would live in New York.

When Guido got home, his apartment seemed dim and airless to him. He turned on the lights, opened the window, and let the cool, wet breeze float in. He felt not unhappy, but lifeless and dismal. He did not feel lonely or wretched, but only pointless. He poured himself a glass of brandy and sat by the window. He was not, he realized, dying of love. He was simply lifeless without its object. What he felt about Holly was not obsession, but enrichment. Without Holly, his life was worth something, but not all that much. Holly was the beginning of his adult life. She was the one to whom he was committed forever. Before he went to bed, he picked up a copy of *Le Lai de l'Ombre* and was not consoled to find that

28

Jean Renart had had the same problem in the thirteenth century. He read:

> Once the erring bow was bent
> Straight to its goal the arrow came
> The beauty and the sweet name
> Of a lady placed within his heart.

At the end of the week, Holly called and asked him to come see her. When he arrived, he found her arm in a cast. She was using a silk scarf as a sling.

"I broke my wrist," she said. "Would you untie this knot for me? It took me forty minutes to tie it."

With her free arm, she flipped the hair up off her neck and Guido untied the knot in her scarf. The scent of her shoulder and the proximity of her neck made him almost dizzy. He expected the cast to be flowered, like her china and sheets, but it was only white.

"When did this happen?" Guido said.

"Three days ago. I fell down the stairs."

"What stairs?"

"You know what stairs."

"Holly, you never told me where you were going."

"Didn't I? I was sure I did. Well, maybe you didn't ask. Paula Pierce-Williams and I went to my grandmother's house in Moss Hill. I fell down the stairs. I mean, I tripped over the runner. Paula took me to the hospital. It's only a little fracture, but, honest to God, Guido, I heard it snap. There can't be another sound like it. To hear something break inside your own arm. Every time I think about it, I can hear it and it gives me a sort of electric jolt."

"Why didn't you call me?"

"I said a week, and the week wasn't up."

"But, Holly. You broke your arm. Your arm means a lot to me."

"It means a lot to me. You have no idea what it's like to sleep with a pound of plaster on your wrist."

"I'm hoping to find out," he said.

He rested his hands on the cool cast and ran his fingers across its uneven surface.

"I can feel that," said Holly. Then she burst into tears. "It's so frustrating. I can't tie my own sling, or wash my hair or anything." Then in a voice so small and tearful that Guido could hardly believe it was hers, she asked if he would wash her hair.

"Yes, of course I'll wash your hair," said Guido. "After all, we're getting married. But before I do—I mean before I wash your hair or get married—I want to know if I am washing the hair of someone who loves me."

She rested her cheek against his shoulder, so obviously miserable he didn't press her.

Guido had never washed anyone else's hair before, and he found it very pleasurable. He swirled the shampoo through her scalp and when he rinsed it out under the tap, that glossy hair fell across his wrist like thick tar. When she sat up, her eyes were glazed. She combed her hair abstractly and then put the comb down with a little snap.

"Of course I love you," said Holly. "How could I not? I would never behave like this around someone I didn't love. In fact, I've never behaved like this before."

"Behaved like what?" Guido said.

"Like someone who was going to get married."

"And you're sure you love me enough to get married?" said Guido.

"Don't be silly," said Holly. "Of course I am."

"And what makes you think so?"

"Guido, I can't be grilled on these subjects. I gave you a list of things I loved about you. I told you why I loved you. Now why can't I simply love you and not talk about it all the time?"

"Are you sure loving my eyes and hands is enough? What about my character?"

"I'm just in love with you," Holly said. "I can't talk about these things. Your character *is* your hair. It's all integrated. I don't think about these things the way you do. I just feel things—that's all."

Guido held her broken wrist gently and kissed all the knuckles of her hand. Her fingers felt cool and helpless.

"I love you because you do inspired things like that," said Holly. "Will you tie the sling up for me?"

He tied the little silk knot at the back of her neck and she held her head steady, the way a patient child does.

PART TWO

CHAPTER 2

ONE MORNING, VINCENT CARDWORTHY WOKE up in a bedroom in Sewickley, Pennsylvania, next to a woman he was not sure he recognized. He knew he was in Sewickley—he had been there the night before and he was positive he had not been on an airplane in between. The woman lying next to him had bright blond hair and ruddy cheeks. She wore a cotton nightgown.

Vincent sat up. Recollection dropped over him like a noose. The woman was Rachel Montgomery. She was a friend of the friends who had put Vincent up for the weekend. He had come to Pittsburgh to address the Planning Council on waste and sewage. Rachel had been a guest for dinner on Saturday night. Memories of the dinner were dim; everyone had had a lot of drink. Rachel, he remembered, had been driven over and Vincent had gallantly offered to drive her home since he was more sober than his host.

Rachel was a divorcée, or about to become one, and

she was quite voluble. He had walked her to the door and had been invited in for a nightcap. By this time Vincent was exhausted as well as tight. It had not mattered to him that he had no idea of how to get back to his hosts.

Rachel had sat him down on the couch and begun: her soon to be ex-husband was a banker and was now in Bermuda playing golf with his brother and sister-in-law. Meanwhile, Rachel held down the fort, which had a tennis court attached, with little Hugh, who was three, and Sophie, who was five. In her spare time, she was in love with the lawyer who was getting her her divorce and he was in love with her. They planned to be married when his own divorce came through. Rachel's final papers were in the mail; within the week she would be a free woman.

"Wasn't it nice of Annie and Richard to invite me as a fourth?" Rachel said. She leaned closer to Vincent.

"It's awfully late," Vincent said. "I think I ought to get back."

"Oh, just have one little drinkie," said Rachel. She leaped off the couch and left Vincent alone to contemplate his surroundings. The couch he sat upon was plaid. So were the shades of the big jug lamps and the rug on the floor. The chairs were the sort you see in men's clubs. Each had a plaid car rug tossed over the back. Vincent scanned the room for a gun case, but there was none. Instead there were framed photographs of two little children, Rachel, and a man who was doubtless the soon to be ex-husband, all in riding gear. There were pictures of children on ponies and adults on horses. On the end tables were vases of paper flowers and silver baby cups filled with stale cigarettes.

Rachel came back with two tall glasses.

"It's much too late to go home now," she said.

"I think you'd better give me some directions," said

Vincent. He did not like the idea of being hijacked by a not sober woman or of being a bad houseguest.

"Oh, no," said Rachel. "I just couldn't take the responsibility. It's too late and too dark and you've had too much to drink. You'd get lost. You'll have to stay here. I couldn't deal with the guilt if you drove off the road and got killed or anything."

"I think it's important that you tell me right now," Vincent said.

"Well, actually, I'm not too sure I know," said Rachel. "On account of because the sitter drove me over and now she's gone. The brakes on the station wagon are shot and Aurélee has the little car."

"Aurélee?"

"She's my French girl," said Rachel. "She lives here and takes care of little Hugh and Sophie so Artie and I can go away on the weekends."

"Artie?"

"My lawyer," said Rachel. "You're my revenge on him. I told him he had a week to get on the stick and start rattling some papers. I told him if he didn't get moving, I'd take up with someone else and you're it."

"You haven't given Artie his week," said Vincent. Rachel had begun to loom at him. "Why can't Aurélee drive me home in the little car?"

"Aurélee drove somewhere to watch the hawks migrate. This is the week they migrate somewhere and she went to see it. So she isn't here. Besides, a little revenge will do me good."

She sat up straight and Vincent noticed that she was quite a large package. Her cheeks were ruddy. Her pink scalp gleamed through the part in her bright blond hair. She looked positively overheated by her own good health. She was wearing a kilt, which Vincent had trouble distinguishing from the couch. He gulped his drink and remembered nothing until the morning, when he remembered a great deal, and realized that he was massively hung over.

He was staring out the window calculating his terrible remorse when Rachel was suddenly sitting beside him.

"Either you're a real gent or a dud avocado or you can't drink worth a damn," she said.

Vincent held his head slightly to the side. Upright, he felt as if someone were stabbing him. "What does that mean?" he whispered.

"It means you didn't come across," Rachel said. "You can't imagine how put out I am."

This information filled Vincent with relief. He believed that sex was involved with destiny. Had anything happened between him and Rachel, he would have dutifully gotten on a plane every weekend to see her until she got sick of him.

"What a damned shame," Rachel said. "I hate missed chances." She consulted her bedside clock. "If Aurélee were here, we'd have time for a little quick action, but she isn't. It's too late now. It's time for breakfast. You can use my toothbrush unless you have foot-and-mouth disease. There's a guest toothbrush in the guest bedroom but I don't want you trotting all over the house. Artie's electric razor is hidden in back of the baby powder. The towels are in a cupboard under the sink. Now, when you come down to breakfast, please don't say anything compromising to little Hugh and Sophie. They have conflicted images about male authority."

Little Hugh and Sophie were delicate, goggle-eyed creatures with soft, curly hair. Clearly they took after their father. Vincent found Rachel and her children in the breakfast nook—a yellow room with French windows that looked out over the tennis court. Little

Hugh was patting his English muffin with his fist and singing to himself. Sophie was eating oatmeal, but when Vincent appeared he absorbed all of her attention. She continued to eat, but the spoon landed in the vicinity of her cheek.

"Good morning," said Vincent, sitting down. Sophie stared and waved her spoon. Gooey droplets of oatmeal fell on Vincent's lap. Little Hugh continued to sing and flatten his muffin with his fist.

"Say good morning to Mr. Cardworthy, children," said Rachel.

"You're not Artie," said Sophie.

"That's right. I'm Vincent."

"What's a Vincent?" Sophie said.

"Vincent is a man's name," Vincent explained.

"Are you a man?" Sophie asked.

"Yes," said Vincent.

"Then prove it," Sophie squealed. She giggled violently. The spoon fell to the floor and landed on Vincent's shoe.

"That's quite enough," said Rachel. "Go into the kitchen and get some toast." Sophie skipped into the kitchen, but little Hugh came over to inspect. He stood next to Vincent and rested his head on Vincent's knee. He was drooling. He looked deeply into Vincent's eyes and then departed, leaving two buttery smudges on Vincent's trousers.

Rachel handed him a muffin and a cup of coffee. "It's so hard to know if they're in the oral or anal stages these days." She sighed and drank her coffee. While Vincent was finishing his breakfast, she called his host for directions and then sent Vincent on his way.

"Artie called while you were in the shower," Rachel said. "So you'd better hightail it out of here. I do hope you didn't leave any traces of yourself anywhere.

38

Children, come and say goodbye to nice Mr. Cardworthy."

Vincent had lived in New York for almost three
years. For two and a half, he had been a trouble-
shooter for the Board of City Planning. This Board
was not attached to any city—it was a think tank for
urban study. Vincent was its crack expert on garbage
—production, removal, potential dangers and uses,
conservation, and politics. Garbage, at the Board of
City Planning, was not called garbage. It was called
"nonproductive ex-consumer materials." As trouble-
shooter he had been on the road, addressing city
councils, government agencies, and sanitation con-
ferences. His apartment in New York was rather
monastic as a result, as was the rest of his nonworking
life. Most of his free time, of which there was very
little, he spent with Holly and Guido at whose wedding three years ago he had been best man.

After the publication of Vincent's last two papers,
the Board had decided that he was too valuable to run
around the country. Thus one of Vincent's underlings
became the trouble-shooter. Vincent stayed in New
York and was rented out to the government on special
occasions.

Now that he was more settled, Vincent had found
himself a romantic entanglement—one that was in no
way productive, joy-producing, or oriented toward the
future. Her name was Winnie Minor and she was
married to a stockbroker named Henry whom she
called "Toad" or "the Toad." All of Henry's friends
called him by this name, she had explained. She had
ambled into the Board one day to attend a seminar on
Urban Education. Winnie was a reading evaluator at
Tift Memorial High School, which was famous for its

basketball team and its low reading scores. She was having a little trouble compiling some data, so Vincent, who had a little free time, offered to help her plan a computer program. They met under the normal curve, Vincent said.

Guido and Holly had met Winnie once and both were alarmed. Holly thought Winnie was the worst of what she called "Vincent's vacuous no-shows" and Guido thought Winnie was the living symbol of something terrible in Vincent's life. Winnie was myopic, but even with her glasses, which she wore reluctantly, her face was so empty of expression that nearsightedness seemed a more animated and interesting condition. She wore the sort of clothes the Queen Mother wears to go trout fishing—tweeds and pearls.

Vincent was not in love with Winnie and he did not find her endearing. She was not in love with Vincent and never seemed very glad to see him. Nevertheless, they conducted what Winnie called their "hidden moments." These occurred when the Toad was away on business or had devoted his evening to squash. The only positive sign Guido could detect in this was that Vincent seemed actually unhappy, and unhappiness in the optimistic Vincent was a good thing, Guido felt.

Vincent *was* unhappy. The incident with Rachel Montgomery had truly horrified him. What he had thought of as a silly, carefree social life had taken a turn toward the indicative, and what this indicated depressed him. Was he fated to be silly forever? Was it his destiny to fall in with married blond girls for the rest of his life? Did he have a tragic flaw? Was his luck the residue of his own design? Vincent began to consider his romantic conduct. He was unused to this form of thought. It turned his conception of the world upside down. He continued to see Winnie when the Toad's schedule permitted, but he did so with a sinking heart. When he dialed her number, he gritted his teeth, as if she were a form of penance. Then he celebrated his birthday with Holly and Guido. This warm and happy evening left him miserable once he was home alone. Holly and Guido had just the sort of apartment Vincent had imagined: it was on the tenth floor of an old building and it looked like a little French country house in the sky. Holly cooked his favorite meal and Guido poured his favorite wine. After dinner, they sat before the first fire of the autumn eating apples and drinking brandy. Vincent wanted to stay forever. When he left, he felt that domestic happiness was forcing the extra man out the door and onto the lonely streets.

His heart was further burdened by a discovery at the Board of City Planning. Now that Vincent had stopped traveling, he had time to investigate his colleagues. One morning, Vincent had discovered a girl named Misty Berkowitz. He found her sitting in her office, slumped over her old-fashioned calculator stirring her coffee with a fountain pen. She had amber-colored hair that fell into her eyes and small gold spectacles that slipped down her nose. She looked bored and misanthropic. The sight of her caused Vincent's heart to leap in an unexpected manner. He poked his head into her doorway and said good morning in a cheery fashion. Misty Berkowitz looked up.

"Get the hell away from me," she growled.

Later, she came to his office to apologize.

"It's hell in the morning," she said. Vincent was about to begin a conversation, but Misty Berkowitz had vanished.

After that exchange, Vincent found himself looking for her and he frequently found her. Her normal expression, he observed, ranged between the scornful and the malevolent, although Vincent had once caught her off guard. She was staring out the window of her office and did not know that she was being observed. In repose, Vincent noted that she was very pretty. She never smiled, that Vincent could see. In fact, she appeared to spend her life in a sort of tear. In the morning, she stormed into her office wearing a green suede coat that she threw onto a chair. When she was working, she muttered to herself, broke pencils, and threw them on the floor. She often swore horribly. When she condescended to bid Vincent good morning, she did so in a hostile whisper.

By snooping around the personnel office, Vincent discovered that Misty came from Chicago, had been educated in Chicago, and had taken an advanced degree at l'École des Hautes Études in Paris. Her field of study was linguistics and she had been hired by the Board to coordinate their Urban Language Information Unit. At present, this unit was studying the effects of urban life in New York City on the Spanish spoken by resident Hispanics. Her date of birth was not on her employment form but on a form not available to his prying. He calculated that she was in her late twenties. Since she was much too forbidding to talk to, Vincent kept this information to himself and carried it around like a secret weapon.

Meanwhile, his hidden moments with Winnie continued, except that there were fewer of them. When they occurred, they found themselves not at Vincent's bare apartment, but at the movies or a basketball game. He began to function as Winnie's baby-sitter and if she missed the more physical of their hidden moments, she did not say.

Vincent was not brash, for all his optimism. Around women, he had a certain hearty shyness and he usually planned carefully his mode of approach. But he surprised himself one day, when, passing Misty

Berkowitz's office, he walked right in and asked her to have lunch with him. She said yes. Since Vincent had not expected to ask her for lunch, he had no plan to cover her acceptance. At lunch, the true folly of his action was displayed for him.

"Why did you ask me out for lunch?" Misty said.

"Do I have to have a reason?"

"Yes."

"I find you very appealing. Is that enough reason?"

"No," said Misty.

"Well, you intrigue me. Is that better?"

"No."

"Look," said Vincent. "Do you know any words of more than one syllable?"

"Yes."

"I see," said Vincent. "Why can't I simply take you out for lunch?"

"Behavior is no accident," said Misty. "People have reasons for what they do. Besides, if you wanted some appealing girl, why didn't you go down to the PR department? It's loaded with appealing types."

"I don't want any of those appealing types," he paused. "I wanted you."

"Oh, yeah?" said Misty. "What are you going to do when you get me?"

"Well, take you out for lunch," said Vincent.

"Really? Well, I don't permit myself to be taken out for lunch."

"Is that some sort of militant stand?"

"No," said Misty. "I'm just not that sort of girl. I don't go in for all that adorable socializing. I think it's stupid and disgusting."

"I see," said Vincent. "You're not very nice, are you?"

"No," said Misty.

The next day Vincent decided to try again.

43

"Will you consider another lunch with me?" he said. "Fifty-fifty, of course."

"Okay."

"Are you sure?"

Misty said, "I'm always sure, if I say I'm sure."

This lunch was considerably more friendly. During the course of it, Vincent learned that Misty spoke French, Russian, and German and that she read Amharic. She had also studied Portuguese and Xhosa.

"What's that?" Vincent asked.

"I learned it in a linguistics class. When I get enough money to get out of this dump, I'm going to go where they speak it and speak it."

"Where do they speak it?"

"Africa," said Misty.

"Well, now," said Vincent. "Is Misty your real name, or is it short for something?" She had given only her initials on her personnel form—A. E. Berkowitz.

"It's real," said Misty.

"How did you get a name like that?"

"Because my mother is a jerk," she snarled.

"And why do you find your colleagues so disgusting?"

"Look at them," said Misty. "They *are* disgusting. So clean. So gentile. So comfortable. So well fed. Rich people make me sick."

At the end of the day, Vincent found himself alone in the elevator with Misty. At this point, he was a little terrified. Was he disgusting, clean, gentile, comfortable, and well fed? Did he make her sick too?

They walked out of the building together and because it was a snappy autumn day, they kept walking. Vincent wondered if she minded being escorted, but he felt that if he asked, she would tell him to go away. But she did not tell him to go away. She was, in fact, almost sweet. Being sweet meant that she did not attack him outright and it occurred to Vincent that perhaps he and Misty might be friends. He had never had a woman friend before. Of course, their dealings had not been precisely friendly, but then Vincent had never had a lunch partner like Misty, or any other sort of partner like her.

Misty lived on a tree-lined street near the Museum of Natural History. It was clear she was not going to invite him in. Instead, they stood by the steps continuing their conversation about the realities of statistical data. He walked her to the doorway. She looked straight into his eyes and smiled. It was more on the order of a grin than a smile, but it lit up her face.

"You know," she said, "you're sort of a goop, but you're awfully smart."

Vincent felt some unstoppable impulse snake its way up his spine. He took Misty Berkowitz by the shoulders and kissed her on the lips. Then, horrified by what he had done, he muttered an apology and dashed off down the street.

That night was one of the Toad's nights away, and Vincent had committed himself to spending the evening with Winnie. So as not to have to talk to her, he took her to a basketball game, but she insisted on having everything explained to her. Vincent missed precious minutes of brilliant defense explaining to Winnie the loose-ball foul, the twenty-four-second violation, goal tending, and the full court press. This helped him to stop thinking constantly about the feel of Misty Berkowitz's lips and the clean, sugary scent of her hair. During the crucial last minute of the game, Winnie tapped Vincent on the shoulder.

"Which team is which?" she said into his ear. Vincent explained.

"Well, how come each chases after a different fellow?" said Winnie. "I mean, number four was chasing after number nineteen and now four is chasing twenty-one and that fellow seven is chasing nineteen."

"That's called a switch," said Vincent. "Now please shut up. There are six seconds left in this game."

"Well," said Winnie, "I mean, don't they get confused or lost?"

The buzzer went off. The game was over. Vincent took Winnie by the arm and steered her up the bleacher to the escalator. There he was confronted by the sight of Misty Berkowitz arm in arm with a tall, skinny young man. She was laughing. Vincent had never seen her laugh. She looked very beautiful, and he had never seen her look beautiful before. Then she caught his eye. For a brief moment their eyes locked. She gave him a look that combined contempt and scorn. Then she and her companion jumped on the escalator and disappeared into the crowd.

The next day was Friday, and Vincent was beside himself. He cowered in the office in dread of being shot that look of pure loathing. He hid himself successfully but at lunchtime he felt as if his head was being boiled and he slunk down the hall on his way out to Guido for some consolation. Misty's office was empty when he passed it.

Guido was not much in the mood to give comfort. He had problems of his own. These problems concerned the Magna Charta Foundation.

During his first year at the Foundation, he had worked under his Uncle Giancarlo, who had shown him the ropes. For two years, Guido had been on his own and the Foundation showed every sign of renewed life and vigor. The projects to which the Foundation gave money became worthier and more noble. It had been noted in art journals that Magna Charta was shaping the cultural landscape. Guido assumed this was a reference to his interest in civic beautification although he kept up with the Foundation's practice of giving money to what Uncle Giancarlo called the lone artist. The Foundation gave money to muralists for work in city buildings and schools, to churches that wished to restore gargoyles, to stonecutters seeking to decorate the facades of town houses, to architects restoring grange halls, to landmark preservation groups, and to sculptors who wanted to put chrome boxes in front of corporate headquarters as well as more traditional artists who cast bronze monumental statuary of local heroes. In addition, money was given to novelists, poets, painters, tapestry weavers, and potters. All of this was under Guido's care, except for matters of pure money, which were overseen by a board of trustees of which Guido was nominal head. The rest were bankers and investors who knew how to add and subtract. *Runnymeade,* the Foundation magazine, had begun its life as a glossy booklet for subscribers to the Foundation. Uncle Giancarlo had decided to make it income-producing, but he had failed. Under Guido it flourished. It was sold to students, bookstores, libraries, and museums. It was also sold in the lobbies of fancy hotels and, Guido learned, was favored in the offices of college presidents, expensive dentists, and heart specialists.

Guido had not only taken over the stewardship of *Runnymeade* and the Foundation. He had also inherited an English girl of porcelainlike beauty who had been Uncle Giancarlo's secretary. Her name was Jane Motherwell. How Uncle Giancarlo had put up with her Guido could not imagine. Jane spilled coffee on his letters, had a ten-minute attention span, spent the large amount of spare time she found for herself filing her nails or out of the office having her hair cut. When she was not out, she was in making innumerable personal telephone calls during which she refused to answer her buzzer. Furthermore, she was surly. Guido took this problem to Uncle Giancarlo, who explained. Jane Motherwell had been hired to replace old Mrs. Trout, who had been Uncle Giancarlo's right hand for many years. She had retired at sixty-five, and Uncle Giancarlo, who decided he would retire at seventy, had hired Jane. "At my age," said Uncle Giancarlo, "beauty means far more than mere efficiency."

On the day that Vincent turned up full of gloom, Jane had just quit, leaving Guido with a ringing telephone that went unanswered, a stack of unopened letters, and a book filled with correspondence Guido had dictated weeks ago. This was in shorthand, which Guido could not decipher. Guido felt frazzled. He realized that he had gotten used to Jane, in the way you get used to constant shooting pains, and he was puzzled now that relief had set in.

"I'm in big trouble," said Vincent.

"Look, do you think you can figure out how this dictating machine works?" said Guido. "What happened? Did the Toad find out about you and Winnie and try to do you in with a squash racket?"

"It's not Winnie," said Vincent, tinkering with the machine. "I'm not going to see her anymore. I told her that last night. She didn't care. Look, Guido, this machine seems to be backward. You press the button that says replay, then start, then record. No, that's wrong. Now I've erased everything on the tape. Sorry. But if you push start first, that makes it rewind to the beginning. Where did you get this from?"

"Oh, throw it out. Uncle Giancarlo got it at a discount a million years ago. What's your problem if it isn't Winnie?"

"I've been behaving oddly," said Vincent. "Yesterday I kissed a girl."

"You do that all the time," said Guido. "That isn't odd. Christ, will you look at this notebook of Jane's?

48

There are three weeks of untyped letters. You don't read shorthand, do you?"

"I didn't expect to kiss this particular girl. It was the last thing on my mind," said Vincent. "Now I feel rotten. I took Winnie to the basketball game last night and the girl I kissed was there with some man and she looked at me as if she hated me. Of course, she often looks like that."

"Who is this girl?" Guido said.

"She works at the Board. She's a linguist and she's very nasty to me."

"That's a step," said Guido. "Most of your other girls didn't seem capable of any human action."

"She's full of human action," said Vincent. "Her name is Misty Berkowitz and she hates everything."

"Misty?"

"Do you think that's a bad sign?" Vincent said. "She says it's her real name and claims that it's her name because her mother is a jerk, but it isn't her real name. Her initials are A.E."

"I still don't see what your problem is," said Guido.

"I walked her home," said Vincent. "Then I kissed her. Then I have to run into her with Winnie on my arm. She was with someone. They were laughing. They were probably laughing at me."

Guido was about to accuse Vincent of childishness, but he stopped himself. He had never seen Vincent so emotional. He could remember Vincent being troubled by women, or bothered by them, or made to feel guilty on their account, but he had never seen Vincent agitated by a girl. The tail of his shirt hung below his jacket. His loosened tie hung to one side. His hair looked as if he had spent the morning running his hands through it. This made Guido feel very old and wise. He felt that Vincent was about to have his heart broken at last and that he would be a bad friend to stop it. Vincent needed to have his heart broken. A go-round with a mean girl might teach him a thing or two that his experiments in vacuity had never provided. A broken heart, Guido thought, was not the worst thing that can happen to an intelligent man who makes stupid choices in love. And besides, Guido believed that Vincent had never been in love. Now he was displaying all the signs: agitation, odd behavior, unplanned kisses, and gloom.

"Why don't you find out?" he said, kindly.

"Find out what?" Vincent said.

"If she was laughing at you."

"You think I should?" said Vincent. "Maybe I should. What a wonderful idea. That's what I'll do. Okay. I'm off." And he bounced out of the office leaving Guido feeling like a father who has sent his young son out into the world for the first time.

Vincent sat in his office, feeling worse and worse. He had seen Misty out of the corner of his eye and what had looked like a wonderful idea now seemed complicated and risky. Being a man of reflection looked good to Vincent. Guido, in his shoes, would have sat around and brooded all day but this was not Vincent's style. Wasn't he a man of action? He picked up the receiver, then put it down. What was he supposed to say?

"Misty, I want you to come and have a drink with me," he said out loud. He cleared his throat and then said it again, looking around sheepishly to see if anyone passing his office had heard.

He picked up the telephone and dialed Misty's office number.

"Misty. This is Vincent. Vincent Cardworthy. I want you to come and have a drink with me, after work, I mean. That is, if you don't have another engagement."

"I don't drink," said Misty.

"Well, come out and have a glass of milk."

50

"I don't drink milk."

"I see," said Vincent. "Well, do you have other plans?"

"No," said Misty.

"Does that mean you will have a drink with me?" said Vincent.

"No."

Vincent's head was now leaning heavily on his hand. He had never felt so miserable in his life.

"Would you consider dinner?" he said.

"Yes," said Misty.

"I don't understand," said Vincent. Relief flooded his muscles the way morphine does. "How come you'll have dinner if you won't have a drink?"

"I don't drink," said Misty. "And I hate bars."

They sat in a restaurant around the corner from Misty's apartment. Misty was investigating the table-cloth and Vincent was staring at his whisky. Neither of them had spoken except to the waitress, who took their order. Vincent took this silence as a good sign— of what he was not sure. Among the things that Misty said she hated was small talk. This made things some-what difficult for Vincent, who was used to small talk with women. He decided to make the first move by saying the first thing that came into his head.

"I'm sorry to have bothered you," he began.

"Bothered me?" said Misty.

"Calling you on the intercom and all."

"What all? What bother?"

Vincent took a deep breath. "It's just a figure of speech," he said.

"I hate figures of speech," said Misty calmly.

Vincent took another deep breath and pressed on.

"What I mean to say is, I'm sorry to have kissed you like that yesterday."

Misty lifted her eyes from the tablecloth. The most remote flicker of a smile crossed her lips.

"Is that really what you mean to say?" she said.

"I thought it was," said Vincent.

"Think again," said Misty. The flicker had turned into a real smile, a smile that looked almost warm. That, of course, was an excellent sign. "Did you actually drag me out to dinner to tell me that you didn't mean to kiss me?" She was still smiling.

"I'm sorry," said Vincent. "I was just being conversational."

"Conversational about *kissing?*" said Misty. "Very interesting."

"What I meant to say is that I wanted to kiss you, but I didn't mean to."

"Well, that certainly clears things up," said Misty. "You and I seem to have very different ideas about intent *and* about kissing."

"I mean, you can't just go around kissing people," said Vincent.

"You did," said Misty. She looked at him thoughtfully. "You know what?" she said.

"And furthermore," interrupted Vincent, "I want to know if that fellow I saw you with last night . . . I mean, I was wondering who he was."

"You were wondering?" said Misty. "You know what the trouble with you is? You're smart but in all the wrong ways. First you kiss me. Then you say you didn't mean to. Then you run into me with some nearsighted woman on your arm and *then* you want to know who was that fellow you saw me with. I ask you."

Relief left Vincent quickly. What a dark mistake his life had been. Misty looked very calm and cool. There was no particular expression on her face. Was it a good sign that she had noticed Winnie's myopia or was it simply ammunition gathering? Her calmness was extremely forbidding. He decided, since he could not figure out what else to do, to continue being the fool he was.

"The girl you saw me with last night is a sort of casual friend," said Vincent. "Or rather she was."

"Is 'casual friend' a figure of speech too?"

"I used to sleep with her," said Vincent. "For no good reason."

"I'm not interested in your disgusting social habits," said Misty.

"She's married to a fellow called Toad."

A huge smile lit Misty's face.

"Toad," she said. "How adorable. Why is it that you upper-class types always name yourselves after reptiles?"

"Amphibians," said Vincent. "Now, who was that man?"

"I am under no obligation to tell you anything," said Misty.

"I told *you*," said Vincent. "It isn't fair."

"No?" said Misty. "Well, here's a revelation for you. You don't have to be fair in this world."

"I'll pay you to tell me," said Vincent. He pulled his wallet out of his jacket.

"My goodness," said Misty. "You really are far gone. Well, okay. That man was my cousin Stanley, who is nineteen years old."

They sat in silence. A waitress brought them each a plate of spaghetti. Vincent had no appetite, but Misty dug in.

"You ought to eat your dinner before it gets cold," said Misty.

"I will," said Vincent, but he didn't pick up his fork. All the clichés about confusion had been created for him, he felt. He was all at sea. He was adrift, a man without an anchor.

Misty ate daintily, twirling her spaghetti neatly

around her fork. When she lifted her wineglass, he noticed that her hair was the same amber color as the wine. She had light brown eyes. He noticed that in candlelight she took on the color of an apricot. She had small delicate hands and pale, oval nails. Her only jewelry was a plain gold watch.

"The trouble with you," said Misty, "is that you're so committed to being polite and doing the right thing."

Vincent sat staring at his cold spaghetti and said nothing.

"If you weren't so polite, you wouldn't have had to go out of your way to take me to dinner to apologize for your random behavior."

Vincent looked up. Misty was smiling.

"You should be more like me," she said.

"I should?" said Vincent. "In what way?"

"I am the scourge of God."

Vincent sat still, listening to his heart beat. Misty was smiling again. Her smile revealed to him that his behavior was far from random. He was in love.

"I just felt bad," he said. "About yesterday."

"In order to feel bad," said Misty, "you should have kissed me a lot more."

CHAPTER 3

MISTY BERKOWITZ'S GIVEN NAME WAS Amelia Elizabeth. She had been named for her great-grandmother and her grandmother, but her cousin Michael's mispronunciation had stuck with her. Misty was stoical about her names. She had ceased to cringe at either Misty or Amelia. She felt that all girls should be called Mary and since she was not she would have to endure, although she took a grim, ironic pleasure in the fact that there was nothing misty in her character.

She had come back from two years at l'École des Hautes Études with a strong command of the French language, a trunkload of books, a green suede coat, and a broken heart. This broken heart had been inflicted upon her by an embassy brat by the name of John Bride, who ran an American cinema on the Left Bank. There he showed grade B cowboy movies and police thrillers. During one of her bouts of homesickness, Misty had broken her vow not to see films in English while in France. One bitter winter day, she went to Le Cinéma Américain to watch a movie called

Rush Street Episode, which was set in Chicago. There was no one else in the movie house. She sat through the movie weeping. At the end, she realized that there was someone sitting next to her. That someone was John Bride.

Misty had had two love affairs. Neither had been satisfactory and they had left her with the notion that she was not generally attractive: that only weird, intense men would ever fall in love with her. John Bride was the sort of man who never did. He was neither weird nor intense. He was the sort of man you see walking down the street with a fashion model on his arm. He was tall and cool and had the lean sort of mouth more experienced women know marks a deep sensualist who doesn't kiss much. He was the sort of man who knew his way around women. He was very skilled. He gave Misty a handkerchief and said: "You're an American girl from Chicago, I bet. No one else would come out on a day like this to watch this crummy film and cry too."

Misty was young enough to be stunned. She felt instantly understood. She took the handkerchief and wiped her eyes.

"How about a cup of real American coffee?" said John Bride. He took her through the freezing wind to an American bar and restaurant for coffee and hamburgers, where he smiled coolly as she revealed herself to him. He knew what questions to ask and he probably knew what answers he would get. Had Misty been older, she might have known the mechanics of this form of heartless approach, but she did not. She had never met a womanizer before. The next day he came to fetch her and took her to the Cluny Museum and out to dinner. Several dinners followed. One night he took her out for a drink, in the course of which she realized that her knees were shaking.

John Bride said: "I can feel you trembling under

the table. Do you think you ought to come home with me?"

It occurred to Misty that an adventure was exactly what she needed. Her social life in Paris was composed of long serious talks with young economists and linguistics students and tame, expensive dinners with American boys who were working for six months at Société Générale. John Bride seemed able to x-ray into her desires. She went home with him. At the time, she could not quite distinguish between love, lust, confusion, and longing. That mixture looked briefly like the real thing. As a result, their alliance did not amount to much. It simply turned Misty around. It gave her a taste of what she now knew she was too old for: that high-flown emotional deprivation that is the earmark of hopeless romantic love.

Women did not leave John Bride; he left them. He felt he left them better off—after all, they had had the experience of him. He was not haveable, he explained. He was not interested in relationships. He was after experience.

Misty had always known that her appeal was not general. The general run of man did not want someone as quirky as she was. She had always run with a precocious set who had spent their afternoons at the Museum of Science and Industry as children and at the symphony as teenagers. The boys who fell in love with her at college engaged her in lengthy conversations about Marxism, Freudian notation, and The New Philosophy. John Bride was symbolic of normal man, which meant that he was handsome and at ease with women. He did not engage Misty in long conversations about anything. He kissed her in alleyways. He took her dancing. He told her he found her beautiful, and the most intelligent person in the world is a fool for this sort of information. John Bride stood for

57

all the men Misty felt were out of her range. Suddenly, one of them was by her side, but only briefly.

This affair was intensely painful for a short time. When the pain passed, revelation set in. From John Bride, Misty learned that yearning was a remarkably time-consuming pastime and that it was not especially useful. She learned that a man who was not intense, myopic, afraid of dancing, or unwilling to kiss in public places might find her attractive. She learned that she could flirt, if she wanted to. The most lasting benefit of this affair was that Misty went to a salon on the Right Bank where she was given a perfect haircut. This had been done on John Bride's behalf.

But she was confirmed in her view that she was a special case of one sort of another. Only another special case might truly love her and since those were rare, and Misty was not a compromiser, it was clear to her that she would probably float through life alone. The John Brides of this world were not in fact for her.

Misty's personality was a deliberate creation. She felt she was not unlike one of those seashells that looks elaborate, but is only the housing for a very soft animal. There was no point—and no fun—in committing the imitative fallacy in matters of self, especially when the self you were housing was moved by scenes of ordinary human kindness. It seemed to her unwise to let the world at large know how easily moved she was, so she kept it to herself. Even John Bride, who behaved like a creature from another planet who had come to earth to see how its creatures might amuse him, was unaware of how deep her feelings were.

In Paris she felt that her girlhood had ended. She returned to America surer of herself. One good hurt inflicted by an unworthy but perfectly beautiful man is not the worst thing that can happen to a woman of principle. It taught you about your own weaknesses. It taught you about style. It polished off your rough edges.

Now in New York, she had no intention of falling in love with anyone. She was not and had never been interested in social life as it was commonly conducted. She did not wish to be taken out for dinner or to have a beau. She was interested in ultimates—like passion and honor. The rest seemed tepid and irrelevant to her.

Vincent Cardworthy, however, was another special case: goofy, harmless, the sort of man who knows as much about the life of the emotions as an infant knows about plasma physics. There was a certain sweetness in the midst of his silliness, and he looked like a man who wanted to be played with. Things probably came easily to him, Misty thought. She saw no reason why she ought to be one of them. That she thought about him, that she found the freckles on his cheekbones, his ruddy face, and his ardent blue eyes compelling was nobody's business but her own.

The Board of City Planning had been founded by Hubert McKay, the great urbanist and city planning pioneer. It was to function as a center for thought, work, and action in the matters of cities and their problems. Each year, members of the Board produced books and studies and monographs. Its staff was hired out to the federal government, to state and local governments, to developing nations.

The present head of the Board was Hubert McKay's son Denton, a trim, forty-four-year-old specimen who wore English sport jackets and boots. He had woolly brown hair, big, empty, platelike blue eyes that were much admired by the female staff, an office full of fishing rods, potted trees, and pictures of his children. In addition, he had a terrific backhand, useful for conning tennis-playing government officials and civic-minded philanthropists out of large chunks of money for the Board. Denton had hired Misty for the junior staff and set her to work on one of the lower floors. Now, as the youngest member of the senior staff, she was brought up to the eleventh floor, where she caught Denton McKay's attention. During her first week in her new office, Denton McKay had sauntered in, positioned himself on the corner of her desk, and helped himself to one of her cigarettes. He lit it and exhaled a curl of blue smoke.

"Who are you, anyway?" he said.

"My name is—"

"I know your name. I think I do. Who hired you?"

"You did," said Misty.

"I did? Gee, I don't remember. What did I hire you for?"

"I started on the language of politics study and now I'm on the Hispanic change in language project," Misty said.

"Right, right," said McKay. "Which one is that?"

"It's the effect of American speech patterns on—"

"Yes, yes," said McKay. "Well, how do you like it here? You're new, aren't you?"

"I've been here almost a year," said Misty.

"Right. Well, when you get used to it, come and tell me what you think of it. I like input from the staff."

Four weeks later he was back. He took a cigarette and said: "Now, let's see. You're working on the transport project, right?"

"Wrong," said Misty.

"Okay, let's see. The waterfront improvement."

"Wrong again."

"One more try. That mini study on upper-middle-class attitudes toward mass transit?"

"No," said Misty.

"No?" said McKay. "What, then?"

"The Hispanic language project," said Misty.

"Right. Right. Well, how do you like it here? You've been here a couple of weeks, right?"

"No," said Misty.

"Yes, you have," said McKay. He smiled abstractly and then left.

It hadn't taken Misty long to figure out that the office was Denton McKay's roulette wheel. You never knew where he would land. He wandered down the halls and popped into the first office that took his fancy although he was never certain whose office it was. He was also full of plans. One day he sat on Misty's desk, looked at her with little recognition, took a cigarette, and said: "I've just been down to Washington. Big conference on job rotation. Great idea. What do you think? I think we ought to get the publicity people more involved in the actual work of the Board. Get them into planning meetings. Teach them to do computer programs and stuff like that. Get the research people down to the PR floor, so the entire staff understands everything that's going on. I think the mail boys ought to come too. I think they ought to know what they're mailing. Whaddaya think?"

Misty was silent.

"I'm a big fan of job rotation. Get the receptionists in on it too. Isn't that a good idea?"

Misty said: "I think it's the worst idea I've ever heard. Or close to it."

"Oh," said McKay. "Gee." He seemed crestfallen. He took another cigarette, which he stuck behind his ear, and left. Misty was sure he still did not know her name. When he saw her in the halls, he absentmindedly called her "chicken"—the endearment he called his children and colleagues he could not identify.

Denton McKay liked plans and he liked to change plans. He called meetings of the staff, which were then canceled. He sent around a memo asking each staff member to state the project he or she was working on, but this effort at refining operations was then rescinded. Most of his time appeared to be spent bumming cigarettes from people whose annual income was about a fifth of his own. This offered him some minimal contact with his staff.

His deputy was Roy Borden, a pale man who wore pale pink glasses and kept in his office photographs of the golden retrievers bred by his wife. A great deal of hearty laughter between Roy Borden and Denton McKay covered an essential hatred. This enmity was hard on the staff. Roy Borden issued an edict and Denton McKay quashed it. Projects approved by Borden were held up for McKay's signature. Most of the staff paid little attention unless these things got in the way of their work, at which point they were forced to go to McKay, a move Roy Borden noted and resented. Those staff members who were politically oriented divided themselves into the Borden Camp or the McKay Camp. Misty, who sat in her office and worked, belonged to neither. In fact, she was unaware that they existed until the week that Board members later referred to as "the siege."

Doors were slammed. Hurried meetings were called. Heads of departments sat in the conference room drinking cold coffee and waiting for either Denton McKay or Roy Borden to show up. Walking through the office was like stepping through a mine field, but no one knew the cause of the tension.

One morning Misty made a foray down the hall to find out what was going on. The only person she could think of to ask was Maria Teresa Warner, whose title was "coordinator." All business dealing with Board projects passed through her hands. She and Misty had never had a real conversation, but they had chatted in the halls. The measure of each had been taken by the other and although neither had moved to institute a friendship, some sort of tacit mutual approval had been established.

Misty appeared at Maria Teresa's door. Maria Teresa was on the telephone. She had a cap of dark brown hair, wide brown eyes, and when she smiled she revealed a gap between her front teeth, of which Misty was very envious. Her voice was low and modulated. It was impossible to eavesdrop when she was on the telephone; the modulation turned into a murmur. She looked up and waved Misty in. Then she hung up.

"What's going on around here?" said Misty.

"Don't shout," said Maria Teresa. "Sit down and respond in a soft voice."

"Okay," said Misty. "What's going on around here?"

"Classic power struggle," said Maria Teresa. "Roy is leaning all over Denton. Denton's wigging out. Of course, he isn't normally what you'd call plugged in. It's so stupid and complicated I can't even remember what the issue is. Oh, what difference does it make? This office is run on pure whim."

"What does Roy want?"

"Roy wants Denton's job, is what it looks like."

"Don't you have to have Denton's father to have Denton's job?"

"Not the way Roy sees it," said Maria Teresa.

"How come Denton doesn't fire Roy?"

"Denton hired him," said Maria Teresa. "No one else wanted him to but he insisted."

"I don't get it," said Misty. "I thought the heads of departments were supposed to be advisers."

"What planet do you live on?" said Maria Teresa. "Denton runs this show. He likes to make sure everyone knows it. He likes it that no one ever feels secure around here—or maybe you haven't noticed. All the junior staff sit around shivering. He once told me he thought security was a deterrent to creative work. Then he went off to some seminar in Wisconsin and came back saying that creative work flourished under secure conditions. Can you imagine? And him grubbing cigarettes right and left. Since I don't smoke, he steals my *Times* and drinks my coffee. And as for Roy, Roy is a monster."

"He is?"

"Of course he is. He's been here for two years and all he's done is rip people off. Like Betty Miller—she was here before you. She did all the work on that pilot project on making the local schools independent corporations and he got all the credit for it."

"Do you hate it here?" Misty said.

"Do I have an independent income? Did my grandfather invent something useful like air or thumbtacks? Do I like food and shelter, if you get my drift?"

"I get it," said Misty.

"Oh, well. You know what Eugene V. Debs says: Class war, not imperialist war. I just sit here, boring from within."

Vincent was oblivious to office politics. There was no reason for him to pay attention. He worked in a rarefied atmosphere, being one of the truly creative types Denton loved and feared. Since the publication of a paper on thrift now considered a classic in its field, Vincent had become a star of sorts. As such, he was left alone and the worst he had to put up with was smarminess from Roy Borden and oversolicitousness from Denton McKay.

The office gossip Vincent picked up he usually forgot, but now it was clear to him that something evil was afoot. He was called into meetings that were hastily canceled, or if actually held had a purpose obscure to the participants. He received contradictory memos. He heard muttered conversations in the men's room. For the first time in his tenure, closed doors abounded at the Board.

Misty was not a special case. She sat in the office trying to work, but the uneasiness in the office bothered her. One noon, she was punching at her calculator dispiritedly when Maria Teresa Warner appeared.

"You'd better lay low," she said. "You're in the line of fire."

"Me?" said Misty. "What did I do?"

"Nothing. You're only a pawn in the game, as it were. Denton told Roy three weeks ago to fire some nonessential people. Roy wouldn't do it. Then Denton decided that no one could be let go, so Roy has decided to act, and you're on the list."

"But why me?" said Misty. "What did I do?"

"You don't understand," said Maria Teresa. "This has nothing to do with anything. Denton hired you. Roy is trying to fire three people Denton hired and you're one of them."

"But I haven't done anything."

"That doesn't matter. Roy has decided to make an issue of this so Denton has decided to feed him a couple of Christians, in a manner of speaking. What's a few Christians to a lion?"

"I don't get it," said Misty.

"I can't understand why you can't understand. It's just prep school in the adult world. They're sniping at one another. Denton has more money than Roy and he belongs to better clubs. That drives Roy crazy. I think Roy is one of those boys like Denton used to dump on in prep school and now Roy is trying to get his revenge. Get it?"

"And so I have to worry about paying my rent while those two maniacs fight out their adolescent traumas? But why did he pick me?"

"Just remember what Samuel Johnson said about schoolteachers," said Maria Teresa. "They are men amongst boys and boys amongst men."

"Rich people make me sick," said Misty.

Misty spent the rest of the afternoon in her office with her door half closed. She studied her checkbook and savings account book and she calculated on her machine how much it cost her to live each month. Noises in the hallway made her jump. When she looked around her office, her eyes filled with tears. She loved her work, and where else was a linguist with degrees from the University of Chicago and l'École des Hautes Études going to work, if that linguist did not want to teach? Her work had been going so well, and now it was all going to end. She turned her swivel chair toward the window and stared unhappily at a girl watering her office plants in the building across the street. She was about to cry, but Vincent interrupted her. He looked cheerful and unruffled. One glance at Misty and he knew things did not look promising.

"Will you have dinner with me?" he said.

"You can go to hell. I'm about to be fired."

"Oh, that," said Vincent. "Did you take that seriously? I just heard about it. Denton is on his way over to talk to you. Nobody's getting fired. That was just one of those Denton-Roy ignorant army clashes. Now it turns out that Roy was just having the last laugh. He just quit. Seems he had a big job in Washington all lined up and wanted to make life rough for Denton before he left."

Misty's face went white. A red curtain of fury fell over her eyes. She picked up the first thing she could lay her hands on and threw it against the wall. It was a heavy glass ashtray and it tore a hole in the plasterboard before it shattered to the floor. Then she got up and made for the door.

"Where are you going?" Vincent said.

"To tell Denton to shove it," said Misty.

She was gone before he could stop her. Vincent sat down at her desk and wondered if he would have stopped her. He felt he would not have. She was off to do battle with Denton and he was worried and proud at the same time. This was accompanied by admiration and tenderness. He was seized with love. Sitting in her chair in her office, he felt very close to her, but when he looked around, he realized that there was very little to feel close to. Her suede coat hung over a chair. On the floor lay the shattered ashtray. On her desk was a ceramic dish of paper clips, her calculator, and a stack of papers on top of which was a spark plug that functioned as a paperweight. There were no plants, no posters, no photographs. He lit a cigar. In addition to worry, pride, admiration, tenderness, and love, he also felt guilt. He was so used to the cavalier behavior of people like Denton that it hardly registered. This, he felt, was nothing to be proud of. He wanted to race down the hall and knock Denton's teeth down his throat and save Misty. But when he thought of Misty, he felt that perhaps someone would have to come and save Denton.

An hour later, she was back.

"What are you still here for?" she said, grabbing her coat. Her face was pale and grim.

"I was waiting for you," Vincent said.

"Then get me the hell out of here and just take me somewhere."

She did not speak in the elevator, in the taxi, or in the banquette of the expensive bar Vincent took her to. When the waiter appeared, Misty seemed unable to speak. Vincent ordered whisky and soda.

"What will you have?" he asked her.

"One of those things they have in old movies," she muttered.

Vincent ordered her a gin fizz. Silence descended again until the waiter brought the drinks. This gave Vincent a little time to consider the options. If Denton had fired Misty, if he could not see Misty every day, he would simply have to throw himself at her mercy sooner. If she had not been fired, he had a few months to go before throwing himself at her mercy. He looked at her quickly out of the corner of his eye. She sat huddled in her green coat looking malevolent.

"All right," said Vincent. "Drinks are here. Please take one long sip and tell me what happened."

Misty took a sip. "My, this is disgusting," she said. "Well, here's what happened. I found Denton coming down the hall looking for me. I said I was looking for him. We went into Roy's office because it was nearest. He must have gotten out fast—there wasn't a thing in it. Then I told Denton that he was a son of a bitch and that he may have gotten away with fucking around with other people's jobs, but he wasn't going to fuck around with mine, and that I quit. I said I was quitting because his kind of cavalier ownership, his brand of whimsicality came a little too close to threatening my livelihood and it was clear he either couldn't see the connection or didn't care. I told him I didn't want to work for some prep school snip."

"You said that?" Vincent said. "What did he say?"

68

"He looked sort of sick. He said he hoped I would stay, that the whole thing had gotten out of hand and that no one was ever going to be fired. I told him he ought to go out and get a job and find out what being an employee was like."

"What did he say?"

"He apologized," said Misty.

"He did? *Denton?*"

"Yes. He said he was sorry and asked me to stay."

"And you said?"

"I said I would stay and that if he ever used me as a pawn again, I would either kill him or sue him. I come from a family of pinkos and lawyers. We don't screw around."

"Oh," said Vincent. "That's quite amazing."

"No, it isn't," said Misty. "It's disgusting. The really awful thing about people like Denton is that they make people like me do things like that. Do you think I like behaving that way? Well, you're wrong, buster. That's the worst side of me. He just can't use me the way he does the others. If they want to dance around him, that's their business. I'm not going to be treated that way."

"I think you're wonderful," said Vincent.

"Oh, yeah?" she said. "Well, you would. I'm not wonderful. I'm the scourge of God. Now, do I really have to drink this thing?"

"Yes," said Vincent. "Every drop. It'll do you good."

What it did was go straight to her head. The glasses on the long, mahogany bar began to wink at her. The vase of flowers on the side table took on a deep, rosy glow. She leaned her head back against the plush.

"Maybe I should have another one," she said.

"A very wise move," said Vincent.

"Vincent?"

"Yes?"

"Can we just sit around here for a while and get drunk?"

"A very wise idea," said Vincent. "I'd love to see you drunk. Are you ferocious when drunk, or what?"

"I don't know," said Misty. "Suddenly, everything looks very soft."

"A good sign," said Vincent. He left his chair and slid over next to her on the banquette.

"Don't kiss me or anything," said Misty.

"I promise nothing," said Vincent.

A gin fizz was placed in front of her. She sipped it slowly, her eyes a little glazed.

"Don't mess around with me when I'm in a state," she said. "I'll tell you something you don't know. I'm awfully glad I'm here with you. If you use that against me, I'll kill you personally."

The Magna Charta office was a long, stylish "L." The prints on the walls were mostly Dürers, chastely framed in thin gilt wood. In the anteroom were framed covers of *Runnymeade*. The windows looked out over the roofs of midtown Manhattan and Central Park. Guido's office was a small room paneled with bookshelves. These contained back issues of *Runnymeade* bound in green, books by authors the Foundation had subsidized, and spiral-bound Foundation reports on projects and works in progress. On a long table by the window were the three Peking glass bowls that had belonged to Uncle Giancarlo and went with the office. There was a brass watering can filled with water and egg shells, a combination suggested by Holly to give the office plants a better life. Uncle Giancarlo had been against houseplants, but Holly had brought in a gardenia, an orange tree, and the asparagus fern that had once hung over her bed.

The sight of this fern frequently sent Guido into a fit of nostalgia. In the hallway was a small refrigerator made of fake bird's eye walnut, which when opened revealed a plastic lime, bottles of seltzer, and three cans of shrimp bisque. At the back was a small conference room containing a couch, a long table, and two upholstered chairs.

On Guido's desk stood a framed photograph of Holly sitting near a wall of roses. She looked calm, impeccable, and absolutely gorgeous. It alarmed Guido how often he sat staring at this photograph. On the other side of the desk was another photo, also framed. This was a picture of Vincent and Guido, looking splendid. Holly had taken it one afternoon when they were feeling very pleased with themselves. Their hands were thrust forcefully into their pockets and their heads were thrown slightly backward. They looked like men on good terms with the outdoors—rumpled, handsome, and sporty. Their high spirits had been the occasion of the photo: they had been filled with an almost anachronistic sense of well-being. "If we're feeling this good, we ought to have a record of it," Guido had said.

Between them in the picture, but mostly obscured by the well-cut shoulders of their jackets, was a blur that was Jane Motherwell. Now she was gone and her replacement had not yet been found. Guido was sitting at his desk. He had called a temporary agency to get a typist and an employment service to get a secretary. That accomplished, he was thinking about Holly and wishing he were home.

Guido longed for home. He longed for Holly's dinners. He longed for Holly. The elevator man had told Guido that he was the only man who seemed happy in the evening, and he was. He felt his three years of married life had gone by in a swoon, although the details, like those in great paintings, stood out in high relief. But what Holly thought was still a mystery to him. Although by action she seemed to love him ardently, Holly did not seem to live in the realm of the emotions. She felt, she emoted, and she never gave it a second thought. The complexities of love and marriage were things she lived with and through, and that was that. Guido, to whom thinking and feeling were the same thing, was learning that you might live with someone whose sense of life was not your own. The world and Holly were on excellent terms. It did not flare up and surprise her. It held no disappointments, alarms, or clubs with which to beat a citizen over the head. She had no grand schemes, no secret visions. Her own notions of things were so internal that she barely spoke about them. But for all that, she was the best companion Guido had ever had.

Holly had no ambitions to speak of, except to live nicely from day to day. Since she had enough money to support this one ambition, she devoted her life to domestic genius. She went to the Bronx Botanical Garden for lessons in Japanese flower arranging and bonzai. She took Chinese cooking classes and fed Guido the results. She had discovered that she had no talent for drawing but she did have a real affinity with clay. After a few small efforts on the potter's wheel, she turned out a large black and silver Oriental urn, got bored, and began a survey of Chinese art. She read thrillers by the dozen, Victorian novels, French belles lettres, and large volumes on the subject of art history. It amazed Guido that she knew so much and did so little with it. When they had first met, she had been writing her master's thesis on the subject of Chinese export porcelain. She had been encouraged to publish it. When the subject was brought up, she yawned and said she might some day. Education, she said, was something that enriched your life—not something you did things with. Guido thought of her as a city-state—strong, well-defended, and perfectly self-sufficient. Holly could cook, do needlework, play tennis, and fish. She had studied the Italic hand, the Carolingian minuscule, and the restoration of paintings and china. She could balance her checkbook to forty-five cents, make a perfect piecrust, identify most wild flowers in the northeastern United States, and bandage simple wounds. She could stand on her head, do a swan dive, repair lamps, and knew the collections of most major museums. Guido had once recited this list to Vincent, including the fact that Holly spoke French and Italian.

"Does she fly on commercial airlines?" Vincent had asked.

"Of course she does. Why?"

"Anything short of a transport carrier would crash under the weight of those accomplishments," Vincent had said.

Guido lived happily with the fruits of those accomplishments. Holly balanced his life and made it sweet. But she produced in Guido a violent longing, even when she was in the same room, as if he could never quite get enough of her. At times she appeared to him like a crystal of smoky quartz. You could see through it and into it. You gaped at its perfection. You looked it up to learn how it had been formed. You took it home and kept it as a treasure. It sat on a shelf to be considered in all its splendor, and it never, never revealed a thing about itself.

By the time Vincent turned up for what had turned into a weekly Wednesday lunch, Guido had hired a secretary. The two temporaries had made appointments and then failed to show up. Five candidates had called. One was an actress who said she would be frequently on the road; one was a young man who said he was writing a novel with the aid of a computer; one did not know how to type; another could type but would not answer telephones; and the last did not speak very much English. A person named Betty Helen Carnhoops won hands down. She was a square girl with piano legs, short, efficient hair of no particular color, and green harlequin glasses that sprouted in each corner a gold rose with a rhinestone in the center. She typed ninety-five words a minute, took shorthand, and answered the phone in a brisk, businesslike manner. When Uncle Giancarlo eventually met her, he said, with a sigh: "How could you replace my beautiful tiger of wrath with such a horse of instruction? This is an office that gives money away for the purpose of making things beautiful and now it is made efficient by a cardboard box."

Vincent felt he did some of his best work at Guido's office. He had written several papers sitting at the table in the back. His own office, like most of the offices at the Board, was crummy. The Board was located in an old building whose ornate marble lobby gave no hint of the squalor above. The Board did not believe in certain frills and so the offices had not been painted for many years. Vincent's was a grayish yellow further flawed by the chipped plaster and nail holes that marked previous tenants' attempts to beautify. It was a workmanlike place, but for sheer inspiration Vincent legged over to Guido's cleaner, sleeker quarters.

He bounced in, full of hope and cheer. Guido was sitting in the outer office looking smug and drinking a glass of seltzer and lime.

"I have finally hired a secretary," said Guido. "What's making you so springy today?"

"Misty," said Vincent. "She actually expressed a form of affection for me last night."

"Oh," said Guido. "Did you bring the sandwiches? You'll have to eat fast and then shove off. I've got to get everything ready for Betty Helen."

"You hired someone called Betty Helen?"

"You appear to be in love with a girl named Misty Berkowitz," said Guido, "so shut up."

Vincent hated Betty Helen on sight.

"How could you hire her after Jane?" Vincent said.

"Because, unlike you, I had to work with Jane. You only had to flirt with her."

"This one's awful," said Vincent.

"This one is pleasant," said Guido, without looking up from the proofs he was correcting. "She knows the value of real work. You don't have to get used to her. She has no mannerisms. A pleasant and efficient girl and she's married, so I don't have to endure the fallout of a stress-filled emotional life."

"Married?" said Vincent. "She's *married?* Jesus, who would marry her?"

"You are a physical snob," said Guido. "It's all very well for you to crab, but I have a job to do. It's taken me two years to pull this place together. You have no idea how batty Uncle Giancarlo was toward the end. He got bored and started giving money to people who wanted to wrap the Empire State Building in macramé. He wanted to fund a sculptor who believed that polygamy was a structure and that a small polygamous community in the Southwest would be an earth work. He started running poems in Turkish in the magazine. Meanwhile, I have put out excellent and profitable issues of *Runnymeade* and I did it with no help from Jane. Now I have help. Why don't you figure out how much garbage Betty Helen and her husband account for and leave me alone."

"Who would marry her?" Vincent moaned.

"She's married to a chemical engineer. She makes one call to him a day. It is a brief call. When Jane was here I had unexplained calls to Rio and Paris on the bill every month."

"It's the amount of garbage for one squared," said Vincent.

"Isn't it doubled?"

"Squared," growled Vincent. "That girl is a cup of tainted soup."

"She's *nice,*" said Guido. "I'm very pleased with myself."

"Guido, how can you be so naïve? That girl is a slime mould. She'll sit under the fluorescent lights out here and weird habits will sprout. Believe me, she's just lying in wait."

"Well, she's my secretary," said Guido. "And I think she's nice."

The subject was closed. Betty Helen took a lunch break of exactly one hour. Most of the day she sat behind her typewriter, typing at top speed while looking out the window. She sat straight up in her chair. She did not speak to Vincent and he did not speak to her. To keep Vincent out of her way, Guido arranged their lunches in the back office.

"You might say hello to her," said Guido.

"I nodded my head," said Vincent. "Besides, her glasses glitter at me." He paced around nervously, eating shrimp bisque out of a can. He had forgotten about Betty Helen Carnhoops. He was brooding about Misty.

"We are on the verges of our lives," he said despondently, banking the empty can off the wall and into a wastepaper basket.

"Now what is that supposed to mean?" said Guido.

"We're prime," said Vincent. "We're in the prime of life. Do you still feel like a child? I do. Why is my life so useless? Why am I suffering over some complicated girl who only likes me under pressure? I should be involved in concrete, long-lasting things. Jesus, if Betty Helen can get married and be normal, why can't I?"

"Go talk to the headmaster," said Guido.

"That's just it," said Vincent. "I keep waiting around for someone to tell me to shape up, but no one does. I keep thinking that when I'm older, I'll get a grip on all this. One morning, I'll wake up and be a grownup."

"No, you won't," said Guido. "You'll just wake up and feel tireder than usual and then you'll find that you've run out of patience with a lot of things you thought were normal. Or you'll get lucky."

"Like you," said Vincent. "You're lucky. Look at how lucky you are. Where did I go wrong?"

"I think you ought to haul that Misty Berkowitz over here," said Guido. "I'd very much like to see what is turning you into such a bore."

Getting Misty to Guido's office was not as easy as it appeared. She was too smart not to know that she was being put on display. Furthermore, if she hated rich people, the sight of a private foundation was bound to drive her into a revolutionary frenzy.

Misty had gotten drunk at the bar, whereupon Vincent had dragged her off and given her dinner, during which she had recovered. He walked her to her door, where she kissed him on the cheek. Now, however, things were back to normal. Normal meant that Vincent bounced into her office with a big smile on his face to be met by the expressionless Misty, who looked him up and down and said, "God, what a jerk you are." This in no way put Vincent off. He felt her tone was less snappish and more affectionate.

One day he bounced into her office and asked her to go to the movies, explaining that he would have to stop at Guido's on the way. Misty had by this time heard quite a lot about Guido and she had been waiting for this summons. She knew Vincent had no intention of going to the movies. She found it endearing that he had so little sense of strategy, so she accepted.

These quixotic acceptances of Misty's left Vincent a little dizzy. He did not know quite what to make of them, or her. Other girls sized you up quickly and then went to bed with you. The rest of the time you spent together was spent arranging where to meet and figuring out a way to fill up time. Then you filled up time by going out to dinner, but these events led up to some point. Then, of course, you got sick of each other and that was that. With Misty, nothing seemed to add up to anything. She did not turn him away. She did not, on the other hand, invite him to get closer. She refused to see him on the weekends. This was also difficult to figure out. She did not seem the sort to have a weekend lover and then spend part of her week in the company of another man, but what else could it be? Vincent had decided that straightforward bumbling was not the worst thing in the world in her case, so he asked her. She flew into a rage.

"What do you think I am anyway? Is that what you think girls are like? Well, I am not a girl. I do not have weekend lovers. I do not go out on what you doubtless call dates. Why don't you go find yourself one of those publicity girls who plays squash and goes to the theater since you so obviously speak their language. What an insult."

"What's so insulting about having a lover?" Vincent had asked.

"You must have known some very dim bulbs, Vincent. You must have hung around with some real out-to-lunch types. Is that what you think is normal behavior? You think girls go out to dinner with men and have lovers on the side? What is it with you guys?"

Of course, Vincent did think it was normal behavior to go out to dinner with him and have a lover or a husband on the side. But this conversation filled him with hope. Clearly he was in the running if she thought having dinner with him and a lover on the side amounted to a conflict of interest.

Betty Helen Carnhoops met them at the door. She buzzed Guido.

"Your friends are here," she said.

Vincent walked in, leading Misty by the elbow. He introduced her to Guido. There was a strange, evil gleam in Misty's eyes. Vincent's face was shining. "Isn't this a nice office?" he said.

Misty muttered something under her breath. Then she turned to Guido.

"Vincent says you put out a magazine in addition to spreading the wealth," she said. Guido handed her a new issue of *Runnymeade*.

"I've seen this one," said Misty. She shuffled the pages like a deck of cards.

"You have?" said Vincent. "I didn't know you read it."

"My dentist has it," said Misty. "Can I put my feet up, or would that tarnish these gleaming surfaces?" Vincent found a wicker stool upon which Misty rested her feet. She wore small, expensive green shoes.

"Would you like some seltzer?" Guido asked.

"I'd love some coffee," Misty said. "If you have any."

"I can ask Betty Helen to make some."

"Oh, don't," Misty said. "Please. I'll just have a glass of water if there's no coffee. I don't want secretaries making me things to drink."

"I'll get you some," said Vincent. "There's a delicatessen around the corner." He raced out of the office.

Misty and Guido faced each other silently. There were a great many things Guido wanted to say, but it seemed against the laws of friendship and privacy to do so.

"It's very nice to meet you," he began. "I've been hearing a great deal about you."

There was no answer. Guido looked at her. She was staring impassively at her shoe.

"Vincent often speaks of you," said Guido.

"You already said that," said Misty.

"I suppose I did," said Guido. "I'm afraid I'm not finding it easy to talk to you."

"Jesus," said Misty. "Your pal shleps me over here and puts me on display like Lady Astor's horse and I'm not easy to talk to. I ask you."

"You *are* difficult to talk to," said Guido.

"Only for the first ten seconds," said Misty. "Besides, this is a setup so that I can be surveyed. Well, do you want to have some polite chitchat, or do you want to get right down to cases?"

"I'm far too polite," said Guido.

"Well, I'm not," said Misty. "You look like someone with something to say."

"All right," said Guido. "Vincent is my oldest friend. He's very fond of you. I don't want his heart broken by a hostile teenager."

"Oh, brother," said Misty. "Is that what he says I am?"

"No, but it's what you sound like when Vincent describes all the ways in which you aren't fond of him."

80

"You boys," said Misty. Then she smiled. Her smile relieved Guido and he took the opportunity to size her up. Unlike Vincent's other entanglements, who were large, country, Protestant, and looked vacant, Misty was rather small, urban, and Jewish. And she looked smart.

She sat back in her chair, lit a cigarette, and twirled her shoe around on the tip of her toe.

"I am not hostile and I am not a teenager," said Misty. "And I was not put on this earth to break hearts. Take it from me, I don't hang around with people I don't like. I am actually a very upstanding young woman but it takes the average citizen years to find out."

"Vincent isn't the average citizen," said Guido.

"I'll say he isn't," said Misty. "Well, am I flunking inspection?"

"No," said Guido. "You passed."

"I did?" Misty said. "What was my highest mark?"

"You scored very well in being easier to talk to than I thought."

At this point Vincent appeared with the coffee, which was leaking through its paper bag. He handed it to Misty. He looked positively wiped out by love.

CHAPTER 4

BETTY HELEN CARNHOOPS WAS LIKE A REEF of calm in a bad storm. She functioned as smoothly as a hospital kitchen and she had the quiet, militant presence of a nurse. Her letters were miracles of perfection: she justified each line like a Vari-type machine. Her telephone voice was brisk and without any tone at all. She almost never spoke to Guido except in the line of work and her only topics of conversation were the weather, the office cleaning staff, and Guido's appointment calendar. She got everyone's name right. Within two weeks she knew where everything was. Although she had no opinions on the subject of art and literature, she was a demon proofreader. It seemed to Guido that she had been sent to him by a benevolent Creator, although he sometimes felt that Betty Helen looked upon him and the Foundation as if she were ministering to minds diseased. The fact that she was a mountain of stability made him truly grateful. He felt that in hiring Betty Helen, he had put away childish things forever. Another Guido—a younger Guido—might have hired Jane Motherwell.

As Vincent had predicted, one quirk had sprouted under the fluorescent lights. Betty Helen announced everyone in the same way. She buzzed Guido and said: "Your friends are here." In this way she announced trustees, delivery boys from the delicatessen, tax lawyers, twelve-tone composers, and telephone repairmen. Guido barely noticed. Vincent, on the other hand, picked right up on it.

"Can't you see that Betty Helen has no idea what goes on here?" he said. "She's either evil or lobotomized. Why did she just tell you that Western Union messenger was your friend?"

"It's hard for a normal person to tell who's an artist and who isn't these days," Guido said. "It's the new casualness. Holly says it's making slobs of us all. Betty Helen has the right attitude. Now, for example, the other day, a guy selling office equipment came in dressed like a bank president. Then the guy from the bank came in dressed like a college professor. Then Cyril Serber came in. He's the poet and classicist but he works out with weights. He came up on his way from the gym and Betty Helen probably thought he was from the delicatessen. So you see, it's easy to be confused. She's a nice, ordinary person."

"Ordinary," said Vincent. "That woman is a mutant."

For the first time since Guido had taken over from Uncle Giancarlo, the office hummed efficiently. There were no ghastly surprises, no temper tantrums, no unexplained absences, lost messages, or free-floating hostility. In this atmosphere, Guido learned how much he loved his job. With a sane person to help you, you could plan intelligently. You could expand. Life worked.

He stared out the window less and less. When he did, the trees in Central Park looked like trees in a pointillist painting. He was now involved in the concrete, long-lasting things Vincent brooded about.

Life with Holly assumed the same lovely shape. She was taking a course in floral painting, and when he came home at night he found enormous eighteenth century Dutch flower arrangements on the hall table. She was also involved in Japanese cooking, and the dinners she gave Guido were arranged like landscapes. After dinner, they repaired to opposite ends of the couch, where, with legs entwined under a plaid rug, they read in front of a fire. Life was sweet and rich, like Imperial Tokay.

On Wednesdays, Vincent turned up for his lunch of shrimp bisque out of a can.

"So Betty Helen's still here," he said. "Really, Guido, she gives me the creeps. Can't you get someone a little less efficient?"

"For God's sake," said Guido. "Leave me alone with my Betty Helen. Life is finally working right and you're trying to screw it up."

"I'm not," said Vincent. "I simply feel, like Uncle Giancarlo, that an office like this, devoted as it is to art, should have someone a little more painterly working in it."

"I don't want any of those beautiful flash girls running around here being illiterate, having emotional problems, and ruining my life," said Guido. "Go play with your friend Misty if you're so interested in that sort of thing."

"Misty isn't illiterate," said Vincent. "And she isn't beautiful."

"She's interesting looking," said Guido. "That's always a bad sign."

"Besides," said Vincent. "She isn't ruining your life. She's ruining mine."

"Don't be so melodramatic."

"Guido," said Vincent, "you have no idea what it's like to be weighed on the heavenly scales and found wanting. There are times when I think everything I do offends her. Not only what I do—what I am, or whatever she thinks I am. She says if there's a revolution, I'll be useless. She says I am interested in applying Band-Aids to incurable wounds."

"If there's a revolution, that girl will have to give up her expensive green shoes. Believe me, your Misty is hardly what I'd call one of the masses."

"I just wish you could find someone a little more like her to work here," said Vincent. "To make life a little more interesting."

"My life is interesting enough, thank you. Someone like her would make my life one solid round of hell."

"Well, brace yourself. She's out in the field today and I asked her to meet me here."

Guido was looking forward to another encounter with Misty. He was not sure what to make of her. She was extraordinary, he thought, but he wondered what an extraordinary girl would do to Vincent.

Misty arrived early wearing her green coat and her little green shoes. She put her feet up on the wicker stool and drank a bottle of seltzer.

"So, how are things with Vincent and the hostile teenager?" she said. She seemed extremely cheerful.

"Since you ask," said Guido, "the hostile teenager appears to be giving Vincent a hard time."

"Poor old Vincent," said Misty.

"She's not entirely nice to him," said Guido.

"Aw, come on, Guido," said Misty. "Why should I be nice to him? He has an easy life. From what I gather, girls drop out of trees and fall into his lap. Part of my function is to give him a hard time. It makes him feel alive."

"That's a very serious thing to say about someone," said Guido.

"He'll get over it," said Misty. "Vincent thinks love is when you go to bed with a dog breeder. He thinks there is one way to behave and if he behaves that way everything will work out. If I were a person who behaved in the one way you're supposed to behave, you and I would be talking about the weather, wouldn't we? The thing about Vincent is that he isn't quite sure how to be personal. Maybe all his other girlfriends were the same girl. But I'm not the same girl."

"How difficult you are," said Guido.

"Yes, I am," said Misty, grinning. "But I'm worth it."

"Do you think Vincent is worth it?" said Guido.

"Let's go back to being polite," said Misty. "Vincent has told me a lot about you."

"I don't want to be polite," said Guido. "Is Vincent worth it, or are you just stringing him along?"

"What a repulsive idea," said Misty. "Of course I'm not stringing him along. What do you know? Maybe I love him."

"Do you?"

"Don't be silly," said Misty.

When Vincent appeared, he looked shy, boyish, and overwrought, and he tripped on the door ledge.

Guido was intensely domestic. Like French women who can tell if a bottle of Cognac has been opened in the next room, Guido could tell what was happening at home as soon as he put his key in the lock. As he stood in the foyer, he knew something was wrong.

In the bedroom he found Holly packing a large

suitcase. Her clothes were piled in neat stacks on the bed. She looked up as Guido walked in.

"Are we going somewhere?" Guido said.

"No," said Holly. "I am." She frowned and began to count a stack of shirts. She had shirts in every pastel and color of stripe, made for her by a Chinese tailor who gave her a break on the price.

"Have I forgotten something?" said Guido.

"This is very spur of the moment. I'm going to France."

"I see," said Guido. He was cold with fury.

"You don't see," said Holly. "These decisions come to me very quickly and when they do, I know I'm right."

"Has it occurred to you, since you are married to me, to talk first and act second?"

"Yes, it has," said Holly. "Life has been very perfect lately. It's so perfect I find it a little frightening. I almost can't see it. I think we need an artificial break. I think we need to be apart just for a little bit. I'm afraid that if one of us doesn't do this, we will wake up one morning covered with emotional cobwebs and taking each other for granted."

Guido's face turned very dark. It was not often that he displayed his Italian temper. He thought of it as a tame lion that got out of hand from time to time. Now it was beginning to prance and roar.

"I could divorce you for this," said Guido.

Holly sat on the edge of the bed. The night-table lamps were on, and the bedroom looked like a bedroom in a consoling children's story: rich, warm, and glowing.

"What you mean," said Guido, "is that you are starting to take me for granted."

"You didn't kiss me goodbye this morning," said Holly.

"You were asleep," said Guido.

"I was awake enough to know that you didn't kiss me."

"And you're going away to punish me for not kissing you?"

"Guido," said Holly, "we have a better marriage than most people. We like each other more. We are better friends. We have more fun. We have nicer dinners. But I think we are getting very used to it. Life is simply going on and on. I want to do something daring for us. I also need a little space for myself. I think some deprivation will do us a world of good."

"There isn't any stopping you, is there?" said Guido.

"No," said Holly. "Listen, darling, I know you think I'm being willful. You think I make decisions out of the sky and spring them on you. Well, I do, but not very often. I went away before we got married for a good reason. Most of the time we simply dovetail. I think that's dangerous as a steady diet and I know I'm right."

"I'd like to strangle you," said Guido.

"You're being unreasonable."

"Unreasonable!" shouted Guido. "You're the one who's leaving me."

"I am not *leaving* you," said Holly. "I am going to France for a little while. We are getting very smug and used to each other and I will not have us taking each other for granted. My instinct tells me that this is right. It isn't for me alone. It's for us."

"It's for you," Guido said.

"You don't want to understand this," said Holly. "You want to feel as if you're being badly treated. But you aren't. I feel that our love is very secure—at rock bottom, I mean. I believe in security but not in the matter of love from day to day. I *want* to miss you and I want you to miss me. If you believe in me, let me go. It's only for a little while."

Guido sat on the chaise. Holly slid off the edge of the bed and onto Guido's lap. His anger did not get in the way of her irresistibility. She smelled of jasmine and her thick, dark eyelashes brushed his cheeks.

"Trust me," said Holly. "This is good for us."

By the next afternoon she was gone.

Guido spent the first day of her departure in his office staring out the window. As the days went by, he stared more and more. In the afternoons he became increasingly weary. Often he put his head down on the blotter and took a short, miserable nap. He found himself talking to himself in the mirror.

"I'm not going to be undone by you, or anyone like you," he said. His mirror reflected back Holly. On good days he made plans for their future. On bad days he felt severed from all human contact.

Meanwhile, he had to put up with Vincent, who had become increasingly more agitated in his pursuit of love.

"It's cresting," he said. "Misty invited me for dinner. Do you know, I've never seen the inside of her apartment before?"

"Good for you," said Guido bitterly. He was a little sick of love in its infant stages.

"Betty Helen seems to be helping you out a lot," said Vincent brightly, hoping this change of conversation would engage Guido. It did not.

"I mean, with Holly gone and all, she's a real symbol of dependency. Misty says it says a lot about you that you hired her."

"I will not have Betty Helen made into a symbol of my mental state," snapped Guido. "And I do not wish to hear the ravings of your psychoanalytical girlfriend on this subject."

"I'm sorry, Guido. I was just trying to cheer you up. But Misty says some very interesting things about things."

"I don't want to hear another interesting thing said by a woman," said Guido. "They're all far too interesting."

"Betty Helen must look pretty good to you," Vincent said.

"Vincent," said Guido in a voice of sinister calm. "Get out of here. You have turned into a chimpanzee. Stop gibbering and go back to work, if you *can* work."

"I'm sorry, Guido," said Vincent. "I'm not too good about knowing how to react. I feel awful about Holly. I just don't know what to do. Maybe I should take you out and we should get drunk."

"That sounds fine," said Guido. "As long as you don't say anything."

When Vincent left, Guido canceled all his afternoon appointments and gave Betty Helen the afternoon off. She peered at him, puzzled.

"I don't understand," she said.

"I'm declaring a holiday," said Guido. "And giving us both the afternoon off."

Betty Helen peered at him again.

"This is probably a more casual office than perhaps you're used to," said Guido. "Go shopping. Go to the zoo. Go to the movies. Entertain yourself. Tomorrow will be business as usual."

Betty Helen stood before him with her hands on her hips. Her glasses glittered at him. It was impossible to imagine that face smiling.

"Business will not be as usual tomorrow," said Betty Helen. "There is not one usual thing about this place. I'm not complaining. I find it very interesting.

It just isn't usual. I hope you don't mind me saying this. I like working in an unusual atmosphere. I find it very stimulating. However, I am a very organized person. I have not typed all my letters and if I left work early, I would have nothing planned to do. I like to do what I plan to do. So, if you don't mind, I'll stay here and finish those letters. Now, I would like to say something to you which I hope you won't mind. I am a teetotaler myself, but if I were you, I would go home and make myself a drink. You look terrible."

Guido had never heard Betty Helen say more than a sentence or two. Now she had given him what was almost a lecture. And did he look so awful that it was visible even to Betty Helen? He peered back at her. Behind her glasses was yet another person he did not understand.

Guido did not entertain himself. He had no interest in zoos, shopping, or museums. The thought of going home upset him. Instead he went walking with the collar of his coat turned up. He bought a pack of cigarettes and smoked as he walked. Then he sat on a bench by the river and let the cold wind make his eyes tear.

Holly had him by the short hairs. She might know if the pictures on the wall were just a fraction crooked, but she was Genghis Khan in emotional matters. Was she one of those orderly people who wanted some form of disorder from time to time? Whatever she was, she certainly knew what she was doing. Guido might sit in his office every day and long for her, but not as ferociously as he did now. Maybe he had taken his marriage for granted after all. This infuriated him. How could he be angry with Holly for going away if she had been right to go away? The smooth surface of Guido's life now looked more risky, more uneven. Tranquillity was not a given of life—that was

Holly's message. Guido tossed the pack of cigarettes into the river and pulled a cigar out of his pocket. Fairness of judgment certainly got in the way of temperament. Had he been able to work himself up to a real fury, he might have gone out and had one of those brief not unjolly affairs. He could have prowled around the Frick Collection looking for an adventuresome girl. Without that capability, he was condemned to living in that Holly-less apartment, forced to confront the light, sweet smell of her part of the closet, to grit his teeth over a lonely dinner, and write his Foundation report at the empty dining room table. He would see a few movies he had no desire to see. He would get drunk with Vincent and listen to him babble about his unpleasant girlfriend. There was no one he wanted to have an affair with but Holly. Each day brought him a postcard from her—a gorgeous postcard of some gorgeous place. Today's had been from a castle in Normandy. It read: "Am thinking all the time. Won't write a letter as would rather talk. Instructive to miss you."

Misty had told Vincent to come to dinner at eight. That gave him three hours in which to be nervous and to rid himself of the last remnants of the hangover he had gotten on Guido's behalf. He scribbled Guido a note on office stationery. "Sorry to have wrecked your liver," it read. He went home, changed his shirt, watched the evening news, read the paper, and paced around his apartment. Two blocks from Misty's apartment he realized he was fifteen minutes early. This led him around the corner where he found an open florist's shop.

"Give me something that looks like the things they hang on prize-winning horses," he said.

The florist, a stooped old Greek, gave him an ex-pressionless stare.

"Death, birth, or you got a girl?" he said.

"Girl," said Vincent.

"Yeah," said the florist. "How much you wanna spend?"

"Lots," said Vincent.

The florist disappeared into a back room after look-ing at Vincent in a way that made it clear he dealt regularly with emotionally turbulent men who knew nothing about flowers. Vincent himself knew very lit-tle. About all he knew was that his Aunt Lila had once bred a hybrid rose and named it after her cleaning woman, Mrs. Iris Domato. The florist returned with a huge bouquet of tea roses, snapdragons, and stock.

"Usually you wanna spend this much, you have a fight with your wife," said the florist. "You have a fight with your wife?"

"Girlfriend," said Vincent.

"Flowers help sometimes," said the florist. "And sometimes they don't."

Vincent was almost sure Misty did not like flowers, but he wanted to bring her something huge and showy. A gesture of affection and hostility was just the sort of thing she might appreciate.

It was Friday night. Walking down Misty's street, Vincent thought he heard a violin. It was followed by an oboe and a flute. For a moment, Vincent thought he was hallucinating. As he walked, the music got closer. He passed a brownstone with open parlor win-dows. A girl with a violin in her hand looked out into the street. Behind her, Vincent could see a group of musicians tuning up. A plaque on the brownstone read: The New York Little Symphony Society. The girl in the window smiled at Vincent. She pointed to his flowers and smiled again. Then she picked up her violin and began to play the opening bars of the Kreutzer Sonata.

Vincent smiled and waved at her. He felt moved and foolish. How many other men were walking around the streets wearing fresh shirts and carrying huge bouquets of flowers? He sighed. Love put you under a yoke, the same yoke all lovers walk under like oxen. Love, he reflected, was not at all like science. It seemed unfair to him that there was nowhere one might research except to go to the thing itself. These thoughts brought him to Misty's door. He rang the bell and waited for her to ring back and let him in.

Misty's apartment was rather like her office, except that there was slightly more to see. She was neither tidy nor untidy. She was simply casual. She claimed not to be sentimental about possessions, and Vincent could see that this was true. She had an old blue couch, a blue chair, and a three-legged stool. In her bedroom was a plain bed with a blue and white spread and an oak desk. Most of the walls were taken up by bookshelves. The only decorative objects were a glass photograph of two stiff-looking people, a platter embossed with an ear of corn, and a little glass vase.

"These are for you," said Vincent, handing her the bouquet. She took them without a word.

"Do you have anything to put them in?" he said.

"Probably not," she said. They walked into her kitchen, where on the top of a shelf Misty was too short to reach without a chair was the small glass vase's taller brother, covered with dust.

"That's an awful lot of flowers," Misty said. "Now what am I supposed to do with them?"

"It is common practice to put them in water and

then place them attractively on a surface," said Vincent.

The vase was washed and filled with water. The flowers were arranged. Misty looked at them suspiciously.

"What attractive surface?" She looked over to the table in the corner of the living room which was set for two. "They're too big for the table."

Vincent took the vase out of her hand, carried it into the bedroom, and placed it on a low bookshelf across from her bed.

"When you wake up in the morning, you can think of me."

"Fat chance," said Misty.

For dinner Misty gave Vincent pot roast and potato pancakes.

"It's a Jewish Friday night dinner," she said. Vincent displayed grand appetite, but after dinner any ease that had ever manifested itself between them evaporated. In her apartment—on her turf—Vincent was silent. It was a little awesome to him that she had allowed him this intimacy. He had never thought of a girl's apartment as the setting for any intimacy at all. A girl's apartment was something you crashed into shortly after a first meeting for a nightcap. Then, if the girl had roommates, or a tiny bed, you crashed off to your apartment. Now Vincent felt that he had stumbled into a cloister. He had expected Misty to be lordly and energetic in her own territory, but she was not. She was silent, withdrawn, and edgy. She got up to clear the table, knocked over an empty wineglass, and sat down again.

"This is awful," she said. "I wonder why I bother. See what you get? You get invited to dinner and it's rotten."

"You mean the pot roast and potatoes? They were wonderful."

Misty looked at him sadly. "You're so dumb you don't even know the difference," she said. "Now you're finally here. That's what you wanted, wasn't it? You're here and neither of us has a thing to say. Now you know."

"Know what?" Vincent said.

"Now you know where you don't belong. Or maybe I know where you don't belong. Think of how much nicer it would have been for you if one of those girls in the PR department who wears bright green sweaters and pink shirts and who goes to Bermuda in the spring had invited you for dinner. You would have had salmon mousse and a soufflé and a nice long chat about the people in the office and you could have discovered that your cousin went to school with her cousin."

It took Vincent several seconds to realize that Misty was not being snappish. She was plainly unhappy. She took off her spectacles and rubbed the bridge of her nose. This gesture went straight to his heart. He had never seen her in this condition before and he did not know what to do. So he knelt on one knee beside her and took her hands in his.

"I've had dinners like that," said Vincent. "But I wanted dinner here."

"This won't work," said Misty.

"What won't work?"

"Any ideas you might have had about you and me."

"What ideas?"

"You don't know what I'm like," said Misty.

"I have a fair idea," said Vincent. "You're the scourge of God."

"Well, there you are," said Misty, listlessly. "It won't work."

"I love you," said Vincent.

"I don't believe you," said Misty. "I think you find me sociologically interesting. You like the novelty but it'll wear off and then you'll get bored."

"Look," said Vincent, "is it so awful having someone love you?"

"Yes," said Misty.

"Does that mean having someone like me love you?"

"Yes," said Misty. "I don't get it. I think you think that if you hang around with someone totally unlike anyone else you've ever hung around with, you'll feel all grown up."

"I see," said Vincent. "You mean, you don't trust it. Is that a reflection on you or on me?"

"That's interesting," said Misty. "I don't know."

"Look," said Vincent, "I never have been in love, before you. I never said I love you to anyone. This is all new to me, and you're behaving like a prima donna. Supposing you get bored with me? Maybe you like me because *I'm* sociologically interesting to you."

"I never said I liked you," Misty said.

"That's more like it," said Vincent. "But you do like me, don't you?"

"Maybe," said Misty. "If I do, it's against my better judgment." She got up to clear the table. Vincent leaped up to help her. She washed the dishes in silence and he dried them in silence, hunting around in her cabinets for the right places to put them. They stood side by side at the sink, which filled Vincent with contentment. This, he thought, is adult life and domesticity. He said as much to Misty.

"What a dope you are," she said.

The dishes were washed, dried, and put away. Misty and Vincent found themselves standing in the living room. The air around them was tense again: the tension of inevitability.

"I wish we weren't quite so standoffish," Vincent said.

"Is that the polite way of saying you think we should go to bed?"

"Yes," said Vincent.

"Okay," said Misty. "Let's go."

The next morning, Misty woke to the sight of Vincent's flowers and of Vincent himself, who was lying on his side, smiling at her.

" 'O night, O night divine,' " sang Vincent. "That's my Christmas voice," he added.

Misty considered him, as if she had wakened to find a fish in her bed and was pondering how it had gotten there and what to do with it.

"What time is it?" she growled.

"It's seven-thirty," said Vincent. "I am now going to make you a cup of coffee and bring it to you in bed. You won't like that at all, will you?"

"Not much," said Misty.

"You lie," said Vincent. "I'll bet no one has ever brought you coffee in bed, have they? They think you don't need it. Is that right?"

"Yes," said Misty.

"Isn't life delightful?" said Vincent. He sprang out of bed, giving Misty a view of his long back. His shoulders were freckled and his hair was rumpled.

"You won't be able to find anything," Misty said. "You won't know how to make coffee in a drip pot."

"I am a scientist," said Vincent. "I will not only find everything, but I will make you a cup of coffee so wonderful that you will froth at the mouth with love for me." He sat down on the edge of the bed. Misty, it turned out, was the color of an apricot all over. Gently he pushed the hair out of her eyes and kissed her on the forehead.

"It doesn't take a lot to make you boys happy," said Misty.

"Au contraire," said Vincent. "It turns out it takes a great deal to make me happy. Now, listen, you can be as sullen as you want. I'll be happy for both of us, but I want you to look deep into my eyes and tell me that you are marginally fond of me."

Misty looked him in the eyes.

"All right," she said. "I'm marginally fond of you. And now, if you will kindly heave over your great bulk, I'd like to go and brush my teeth. One scant sugar in the coffee, please."

Vincent made a wonderful cup of coffee. It was one of his few kitchen skills. That cup of coffee surprised Misty. She leaned back against her pillows and drank it slowly. It was little things that did you in, she thought. She did not mean to lean over and kiss Vincent on the shoulder, but she did. This made her cross, so she gulped down her coffee, threw the covers at Vincent, and stalked off to take a shower.

Under the water, she considered her position. Sex, she knew, was something that could not be lied about. Had she followed her true inclinations, she would not have been in the shower at all. She would have been back in bed with Vincent. There was no hiding true desire, so he probably knew it. This, however, did not mean he had to know anything else. Why, she wondered, was caginess so dear to her? Why did she protect herself so closely?

The water ran pleasantly down her back. There *was* something wonderful about having someone love you. Rapture does not spring up out of nowhere. Misty figured that time was running out. A few more weeks of this and she would be a replica of Vincent, announcing her state of love to strangers on the subway. She turned off the water and wrapped herself in a towel. In the steamy mirror, she confronted herself. Love made fools of everyone. It was man's fate.

Guido sat alone in the park. It was lunchtime. The nippy weather was about to break and turn into something more serious. As he sat, the last of the leaves drifted down to the path. His companions in the park were not bouncy schoolchildren or joggers or dog walkers and their dogs. It was too cold for those young executives who meet on benches for a hot dog and a chat. On the bench across from him sat a dejected person of undetectable gender wearing a dress and a riding hat and sporting a thin mustache. On another bench a surly-looking boy—clearly a truant— was feeding popcorn to the pigeons and reading a hockey magazine. And there was Guido, contemplating the leaves that fell in melancholy swirls.

In his pocket he had a letter from Holly announcing her return. This letter neglected to be specific about the date. It was unclear about everything else as well. She said she was coming back and was dying to talk. She was filled with a sense of the newness of things, she said. This quite amazed Guido. He did not expect his precise wife to use language of this sort, but she did, at least on emotional occasions. What *was* the newness of things? Did that mean she loved him over again, or that she loved someone new and now wanted a divorce?

Holly's announcement of arrival came on the heels of Betty Helen's announcement of departure. Her mother in Skokie was ailing, she explained, and she would have to go and stay with her until she recovered. Then, Betty Helen said, she would certainly be back—but when, she could not quite say. Guido felt that everyone was leaving him or had left him and no one would give him any specifics. Everyone, except, of course, Vincent.

Vincent had dropped by on his way out to a business lunch. From the radiance of his face it was perfectly obvious that his great love had been consummated. Guido had said, "Did you have a nice weekend?" Vincent had actually blushed.

"I spent the weekend with Misty," he said. Guido did not respond. "I was just checking in," Vincent said. "To see how you were doing." With Holly gone, Vincent felt that Guido had been invalided, and he phoned every day to see if he was still alive. A few days a week he dropped by to make sure the voice on the telephone had a body attached to it.

"Betty Helen is leaving," Guido said.

"That's good news," said Vincent.

"Not to me," said Guido. "It's only temporary. Her mother is sick."

"That's ridiculous," said Vincent. "She doesn't have a mother. She was cloned off someone's Wellington boot."

"Life is a little nightmarish," said Guido. "What is it about me that makes women get vague about their plans? Holly goes off and doesn't say when she's coming back, and now Betty Helen is doing the same thing."

"It's only a fad," said Vincent.

"Now I'll have to get a temporary," said Guido. "That means talking to more actresses who can't type and Hegelians who can't file."

"You don't look at all well," said Vincent. "Maybe you should come and have dinner with me and Misty."

The idea of dinner with Vincent and Misty

101

sounded exactly the thing to Guido, but, he knew, recently consummated love should be left alone as much as possible. He declined. They smiled shyly at each other.

"Holly's coming back," said Guido.

"I thought she was still hanging you up," said Vincent.

"She is, but she says she's coming home."

"Well, that's good news, isn't it?"

"She hasn't bothered to say when," said Guido.

"I don't understand women," said Vincent. "Even when they do what you want them to do, they're not understandable. You'd think that after spending a weekend with a girl, you'd have some idea of what she thought and felt and all. But not Misty."

They exchanged looks of mutual resigned puzzlement. They both felt exhausted, dizzy, and displaced, like dancers after a long ballet.

CHAPTER 5

THE FORMER HOLLY STURGIS HAD BEEN GONE for six weeks, during which she toured France with her mother, bought four pairs of shoes, and read the complete Proust. One day, she called Guido from the airport and said that she was coming home to unpack her clothes and would meet him for dinner.

"I want to see you in public first," she said. "It's too connubial and old hat in private."

They met at the Lalique, a small ornate restaurant that they had frequented as newlyweds. It was a very brief meal, since neither had much in the way of appetite. They left their dinners virtually untouched, but knocked back a bottle of white wine.

"This place is littered with memories," said Holly. They left abruptly, overtipping. In their apartment, the chamber of Guido's recent solitude, Guido felt moved to deliver himself of a lecture about separations in general and theirs in specific, but Holly seduced him with great love and kindness, which shut him up for some time. Then she brought him tea on a tray. He lay in bed, hogging all the pillows and staring with relief at the sight of her full closet as she went to get a nightshirt. Cohabiting with only part of her wardrobe had been more of a strain on him than he had realized.

"I think it would be nice to move," said Holly. "I think this interlude did us worlds of good and now we should have a new backdrop."

"I'm not sure what you mean," Guido said.

"What I mean is that we have made a break with a certain kind of security. Now we are rejoined and it would probably be a good thing to rearrange ourselves altogether. New rooms, new decor. I would like to get *used* to something again. Besides, I never liked the kitchen."

"What new decor? What kitchen? I'm not entirely sure why you left in the first place. You never said you didn't like the kitchen. You said you did like it."

"First things first," said Holly. "The kitchen doesn't have enough work space. I've been making do, but it's hard to do any really serious cooking. Next, I didn't *leave* you. I went away. I know you understand that, Guido, but I think you don't want to understand it. I do not want to get used to everything going well. I don't want to get used to marriage. It's too serious. I like daily life as much as the next person and I love daily life with you. We could go on and on quite happily but I think you have to interrupt things once in a while in order to get perspective."

"Does this mean that I am going to be tortured in this way from time to time?"

"Don't be silly. Close your eyes and tell me exactly what is in this room."

Guido shut his eyes and described in minute detail every object in the room.

"What's the point of this?" he said.

"Well, the point, of course, is that people get too used to things. I keep forgetting you don't, but I keep thinking you will so I try to keep one step ahead so you can't. If you got used to me, I think I'd shrivel up."

They were lying side by side. Holly's head was propped up with one of the ornamental bed pillows she had retrieved from the closet where Guido, who could not endure the sight of them during her absence, had stashed them. Holly's hair was a little mussed. She wore a prim nightshirt, turquoise earrings, and the gold and turquoise ring Guido had intended as an engagement ring but which had turned into a wedding ring. Perhaps, thought Guido, it was her Oriental hair that made her seem inscrutable. But what did it matter? She was back.

Thus their reconciliation. But even with her sleeping next to him, Guido turned over and over during the night to make sure she was actually there. She always was, her hair nestled against the pillows and one elegant foot on top of the blanket. She was sleeping the sleep of the just and innocent. Her clothes were folded neatly over the armchair that for six weeks had held nothing more inspiring than copies of *The New York Times*.

The next morning she was up before he was, and he found her drinking coffee and wearing his old camel's hair robe. Her eyes were bright with unfocused alertness. She was reading the society page. At his place was a covered plate of muffins and jam. Holly read to him from the paper as if they had never been parted.

"It says here in the people column that a twenty-year-old boy stamp collector has been having a correspondence with an eighty-year-old woman stamp collector and that they plan to be married. Isn't that extraordinary?"

"They'll get used to it," said Guido.

"Don't tease, darling," said Holly, pouring him a cup of coffee. "They probably will get used to it and they'll be sorry. Here's the front page."

Guido barricaded himself in back of the sports page and emerged when Holly brought him a plate of very perfect scrambled eggs with chives.

"I thought I might check out the real estate market today," said Holly. "Just in case there's an apartment with our name on it. It might be nice just to look around and see how good we've got it—unless something better turns up." She got up from the table and put her arms around his neck. "I've got a million errands to do," she said. "I'm going to get dressed. There's a little more coffee in the pot for you and some hot milk on the stove. I'll call you at lunchtime."

With that, she disappeared into the bedroom, leaving Guido to reflect that in matters of the heart, his wife was very businesslike.

It was a bright, cold morning. The sun shone through fat gray clouds, a nippy wind blew leaves into whirlwinds, and the sky, when the clouds moved, was an intense, cheery blue. It was not the sort of weather in which to be perplexed.

However, Guido was perplexed. Holly was as bewildering as ever. He needed time to contemplate her return, but time was not his. Betty Helen had flown off to visit her ailing mother, and Guido was now faced with the prospect of interviewing dozens of unsuitable boys and girls. Modern life was not producing very many Betty Helens, Guido thought sadly. How he would miss that steady, dependable, uninflected presence. Betty Helen was as bland as cream of rice.

At the door to his office he was greeted by a young man who wore his hair in the style of the early John Donne, a three-piece tweed suit, and cowboy boots.

"Can I help you?" Guido said.

"Yeah, I'm looking for Guido Morris."

"I'm Guido Morris."

"Oh, yeah? Far out. Well, I'm Misty Berkowitz's cousin, Stanley Berkowitz, and I'm your new secretary. I'm a present from Misty and your pal Vincent."

"How nice," said Guido. "I've never had a male secretary before."

"I'm not a male secretary, man. I just type real fast. I'm taking a leave of absence from Princeton and I need some gainful employment. Misty thought I should have worn a ribbon around my neck with a little card. I'm the solution to all your problems."

"I see," said Guido.

"Well, you don't look too happy, but you will be because I'm basically steady. I'm a nervous type so I can type about a million words a minute. I can also read Greek and Latin. I'm in Classics, see."

"We don't get very much call for Greek and Latin," said Guido. "This may be a very dull place for you to work."

"I need a dull place, man. I'm trying to let my brain cool out. I got very wired up last semester and I have to cool out."

"Can you take dictation?"

"No, man," said Stanley. "But I can write very, very fast."

Stanley wrote a rapid, legible hand. He made excellent coffee. He loved to answer the telephone because of the groovy voices and he did in fact type like a demon. Shortly before lunch, he presented Guido with a stack of typed letters. All the w's had been left out and were written in an Italic hand.

"Is the *w* key on that typewriter broken?" Guido asked.

"No, man. It's a little device I made up from going crazy typing term papers. See, you pick a letter and then you leave it out and then you write it in. It's a little challenge. I discovered it when I was on ups."

"Ups?" said Guido.

"Speed," said Stanley. "You know, amphetamines and stuff. All us young persons used to do it. My mind was turning into pea soup, so I stopped. But you discover some really weird stuff, like what I call 'the left-out-letter syndrome.'"

"It looks very nice," said Guido.

"Yeah, well, it looks like the key is broken but it gives a sort of personal touch."

Vincent had already met Stanley. Misty had formally introduced them. He had taken this as yet another good sign—meeting a member of your beloved's family. His first night with Misty had been followed by many others. It seemed to Vincent that Misty took this for normal life. Vincent, of course, did not. He had made it a point to turn up in Misty's office at around five o'clock to see if she were free. The first few times, he was formal and abashed. He said, "Can we, that is are you, I mean are we going to see each other tonight?"

This did not sit well with Misty. "Oh, cut it out," she said. "Stop turning me into some sort of social encounter." By these utterances was Vincent's heart made easy. Not to treat her as a social encounter meant to treat her like an established part of his life.

"Well, I figure it's right to ask," Vincent said.

"Oh, spare me your politeness," said Misty. "Did

you think I wasn't going to see you? Do you think I go to bed with any old fellow and then not see him? What do you think this is all about, anyway?"

"It just seems considerate to ask first."

"Spare me your figures of speech," said Misty.

Thus they fell into haphazard domesticity. Vincent asked nothing—if he asked, it might evaporate, he felt. Usually they repaired to Misty's apartment, which was smaller than Vincent's but had pots and pans and dishes. Vincent was himself somewhat indifferent to his surroundings. He had taken a rather grand apartment that during his tenure as troubleshooter he had barely used. Before he met Misty, he had decided that bachelorhood was a form of penance and ought to be rather more wretched than not. He had been in the habit of dining out. Thus his apartment had little to offer in the way of creature comforts. He and Misty visited it when Vincent needed a clean shirt or to pick up his mail.

At Misty's they watched the evening news on Misty's tiny television. Vincent read the paper and drank his evening glass of whisky.

The whisky, he felt, was a definite sign. In fact, it was a turning point. Since Misty never entertained and almost never drank, there was nothing alcoholic in her apartment. A few weeks after their first night together, he was dazzled to find that she had bought not just a bottle of whisky, but a bottle of Irish whisky. Misty said nothing about this, nor did Vincent, who was moved beyond measure that she would actually go out and buy what he liked best.

After the news, they had dinner out, or dinner in. Misty could make pot roast, stew, and omelettes and Vincent had been taught by Holly to make a perfect salad. Together they collaborated on a series of soufflés.

"I like cooking only when it's dangerous," said Vincent.

In the evening, Vincent smoked his cigar and read at one end of the couch. Misty sipped her coffee and read at the other end. This was not romance as Vincent had ever known it. In fact, their first night together might have been viewed by ordinary lights as relatively unromantic. Vincent did not sweep Misty off her feet. She did not wilt into Vincent's arms and say: "Take me, I'm yours." They did not drink themselves into a state and repair to bed in a tangle of bedclothes. They had simply gone to bed as if they had spent a lifetime going to bed together. They took off their clothes and folded them. Neither made a point of noticing the other's trembling hands. Misty had pulled back the covers in a matter of fact way, except that her knees were shaking. Once in bed, they did not fall on each other with incoherent cries. They did not shut their eyes and swoon with unnameable raptures. They lay side by side for a while until they discovered that they were holding hands.

"So. Here you are," said Misty. Her voice was unsteady. Vincent did not take this as a sign to lift her into his arms. He turned over on his side. She turned to face him. They did not smile. Their hearts were pounding. The poet says: "We breathe each other in, from ember to ember." They breathed.

Now Vincent had actually met a member of her family. Stanley had been invited for dinner and Vincent found him very entertaining. In an effort to lock up as much as possible at one time, he put it to Stanley.

"If you're taking off the semester, why don't you go work for my friend Guido Morris? He's in a bit of

110

a jam and you might help him out. And it's a worthy cause."

He was delighted to see Stanley hard at work when he walked into Guido's office. Stanley, who found Vincent's field of expertise inexhaustibly amusing, said, "What's new on the rubbish heap?"

"How's the life of a male secretary?" Vincent said.

"It's far out," said Stanley. "Of course, I've only been at it a few days. Mr. Morris will see you now. How's that? Nice and official, huh?"

Guido was sitting at his desk reading proposals and drinking a glass of seltzer and lime juice.

"What's happening on the rubbish heap?" he said.

"Is Stanley writing your material now?" said Vincent. "How's Holly?"

Guido felt a resurgence of despair. "She's wonderful. I'm terrible. I feel as if I had been flattened by a truck, but she's as adaptable as a thermostat. She says she wants to move. She said something last night about the artifacts of stasis."

"What's that?"

"I have no idea. When she gets like that, I never know what she's talking about. On every other subject she's as clear as glass. I can't talk about it. All I know is that she's back."

"Remember when we were young and everyone used to think that women were emotional?" said Vincent. "I wonder what lucky person thought that one up. It's awful when you realize that the way things used to be is boring but the way things are is altogether strange. All the girls I used to know seem like chaff, but I'm beginning to think a swooning woman might be very attractive."

"By that I expect you mean that your friend Misty is giving you a hard time," Guido said.

"If you mean, is she attacking me, she isn't, but

she's hardly giving me a break. I know she doesn't find me ape-like and repellent, but I can't find out how else she finds me. She's a clam. Oh, what the hell. I'm going to ask her to marry me."

"Why don't you stick your head in a coal stove?" said Guido. "It saves time."

"I love her," said Vincent. "And I'm certain that she loves me. She won't tell me because she says I don't deserve to know. But I'm positive she does."

"Isn't life simple?" said Guido, bitterly.

"In the old days," said Vincent, "I'd pop the question and she'd say yes and then we'd go and do it. Then we'd settle down and live our lives like normal people."

"What makes you think you're normal?" said Guido. "Besides, in the old days, there weren't any Hollys or Mistys. Our trouble is that we don't know how things are supposed to be anymore."

"I don't care," said Vincent. "I'm going to proceed on the assumption that things are the way they're supposed to be and I'm going to ask Misty if she wants to marry me."

"You barely know her," said Guido.

"So what?" Vincent said. "And you're a fine one to talk. You hardly had a long engagement. Besides, you're the one who said that when you're right, you're right. So now I'm right."

"I'll send you the name of a good lawyer as a wedding present," said Guido. "But before you propose, please thank her for sending Stanley to me."

"I will," said Vincent. "But why before?"

"You might not want to talk to her after she's turned you down," Guido said.

Misty sat in her office staring at the pear she had bought for her lunch. It was a hard, unripe little

Seckel pear and the thought of eating it upset her. The thought of doing anything upset her. She sat reflecting on the civil war between her character and personality. One had trapped the other. Her character, she decided, was like the tender stomach of a porcupine and her personality was a bunch of quills. When the porcupine is frightened, she knew, it rolls itself up into a ball to protect its vulnerable stomach from harm. The enemy does not know how soft the porcupine is inside; only the porcupine does.

How happy Vincent would have been to know how often she thought of him, how secretly she doted on him. When she thought of the passionate way he sometimes looked at her, she felt a hot wave of love in the vicinity of what Vincent called her "vestigial heart."

She did not understand how he endured her, yet he did. Perhaps in his militant optimism, he looked through those barbs and saw what she was making such a feeble but desperate effort to protect. Perhaps he would get sick of it and go away. Perhaps she would have to knuckle under and reveal herself.

In the midst of these reflections, she looked up to find Maria Teresa Warner staring at her.

"My, you look terrible," said Maria Teresa. "I came in to ask you if you had any interest in a cheap lunch."

"I'm off my feed," said Misty.

"What an indelicate turn of phrase," said Maria Teresa. "You look as if you're off any number of things. I think I'll have to drag you out of here. You look like your own shroud."

Misty allowed herself to be dragged off to a coffee shop around the corner. She and Maria Teresa were now frequent lunch companions. It was a relief to

Misty to be bullied. Maria Teresa forced her to order a sandwich and a cup of coffee.

"See?" said Maria Teresa. "You were starving. Now, what's wrong with you? Does this have to do with Vincent Cardworthy?"

"What do you mean?" mumbled Misty.

"What do you mean, what do I mean?" said Maria Teresa. "It's perfectly clear. Don't look so alarmed. I have an unfailing eye for these things. No one else would notice. You two are far too delicate and cagey. Of course, you can't fool a delicate and cagey type like me. What gives?"

"Nothing," said Misty.

"What a terrible liar you are," said Maria Teresa. "He's in love with you, isn't he?"

"Yes," said Misty. "Do we have to talk about this?"

"Yes, we have to talk about this," said Maria Teresa. "And why not? You're the only person around here I can stand to talk to. So. He loves you but you don't love him, right?"

"I don't want to talk about it," said Misty, pushing the crumbs from her sandwich around on her plate.

"That's very attractive," said Maria Teresa. "Didn't your mother tell you not to make abstract drawings out of your food? So, he loves you and you can't stand him."

"I can't talk about this," said Misty.

"Oh, my God. You're about to cry. Here, take this napkin, but don't shred it. I'm awfully sorry. I thought it would do you good to talk."

"It will," said Misty. "I don't hate him. I don't despise him. I just don't want him to know how I feel."

"You don't? Why not?"

"I mean, I don't want to have it out on the table until I'm sure of what I'm doing. I don't want him to

114

love me. I don't want to love him. I want to be left alone."

"My, my," said Maria Teresa. "I do admire your distance. If someone loved me, I'd probably pay him. You know what St. Teresa of Ávila said? She said: 'It must be in my nature, for anyone who gave me so much as a sardine could obtain anything from me.' What a pillar of strength you are."

"You don't take this seriously," said Misty. "Well, I do. I just don't get it. Why me? I'm not his type."

"Perhaps he sees into the beauty of your immortal soul."

"I don't have an immortal soul," said Misty. "I just don't understand what makes him so sure he loves me."

"St. Teresa said: 'When I desire something, I am accustomed naturally to desire it with some vehemence.' Maybe Vincent feels the same way."

"Maybe he does. But why me?"

"Well, this may overstep the bounds of our friendship, but here's what I think. I think you're in love with him and you're frightened."

"Is that a revelation from St. Teresa of Ávila?" Misty said.

"Horse sense," said Maria Teresa. "I got it from a horse."

Misty crumbled her napkin into a little ball.

"Please don't throw that," said Maria Teresa, taking the crumpled napkin out of Misty's hand. "And don't start drawing on the table with sugar. I'm right, aren't I?"

"Maybe," said Misty.

"So what's your problem? You should be as happy as a little bird. I like Cardworthy. I wouldn't mind getting a couple of sardines from him. Why can't you just be glad?"

"I can't stand to do anything without a fight," said Misty.

That afternoon, after work, Misty met Stanley in the park. She was exhausted. He was full of energy.

"Working really wires you up," he said. "But not in a hysterical way. That Guido is a decent dude."

Misty was considerably Stanley's senior, but they fit together like a pair of old shoes. They were not precisely close—they were used to each other. This gave Misty a younger person to bully and Stanley an older woman to talk to. Stanley was having romantic problems. He had spent the summer trying to entice a girl named Sybel Klinger to share his sublet with him. She had not consented but Stanley was still trying.

Sybel was a modern dancer who also studied mime. She was a vegetarian and took a brand of vitamin pills that could be obtained only in New Jersey. When not at mime or dance class, or arguing with Stanley about whether or not she would hang her leotards in his closet, Sybel concentrated on her mental and spiritual well-being. Once a week she saw a psychiatrist who believed that all mental distress had its origin in posture. He had recommended that Sybel use the Oriental martial arts as a method of coming to grips with herself. Two nights a week she studied Kendo. One afternoon a week was devoted to T'ai chi. Sybel meditated before each meal and before going to bed. On Saturday afternoons, she sat for three hours with her meditation group. Due to this overcommitted schedule, Sybel's time with Stanley was limited. This was his most compelling argument for her moving in, although Misty could not understand how her cousin could live with such a person and survive. But Stanley's apartment was cluttered with Sybel's possessions—her tatty leg warmers, her numerous bottles of vitamin pills, her jars of kelp, soybean paste, and brown rice. The three-pound leg weights she walked around in to strengthen her calves were hanging over the bedroom doorknob.

The time they spent together was taken up in large part by looking for a restaurant in which Sybel might eat. Walking into an ordinary restaurant was as good as drinking a bottle of poison to Sybel, and her schedule prevented her from shopping for the chewy vegetables she craved.

But it was not Sybel that Misty had come to discuss. Misty was sick of Sybel. She had been sick of hearing about her and one meeting had made her thoroughly sick of Sybel altogether. Sybel had heavy brown hair worn in a braid down the back of her head. She looked moist and dewy and wore smocks. Her whispery voice had a smug, stubborn edge to it that made Misty long to kick her.

What Misty wanted to talk about was Vincent. She wanted to with some reluctance. It is annoying to want your younger cousin's impressions of your beloved, especially when your younger cousin's girlfriend is a simp.

"Boy, I'd like to get a hot dog," said Stanley. "Sybel would kill me. She says you can tell if a person has been eating meat. She says they ought to put a skull and crossbones on packages of hot dogs. That sorta takes the fun out of it."

"Stanley," said Misty. "Sit down on this bench and tell me what you think of Vincent."

They sat down on the bench under a streetlight.

"Why do we have to sit here in the cold?" said Stanley. "Why can't we go someplace nice and warm and eat meat and talk about this?"

117

"Sit down and shut up," said Misty. "This is serious."

"Well," said Stanley. "I like him a lot. I mean, viscerally. He's real smart. Of course, he likes you a lot, so maybe he's not so smart."

"Do you think I should marry him?"

"Did he ask you? Or did you ask him?"

"It hasn't been mentioned," said Misty.

"So what's the big deal?" said Stanley.

"It's going to be mentioned."

"Yeah, well, when it does, give me a call."

"Stanley, you are a self-absorbed pig."

"No, I'm not. I'm your cousin. I don't know. Do you love him and all that?"

"That's none of your business," said Misty.

"Geez, Misto. You sure are strange. You ask my advice and then you won't even say if you love him. If he's dumb enough to put up with you, you should marry him. Guys like him don't grow on trees. At least not in this park. What'd you ask me for, anyway?"

"Because you're family," said Misty.

"Oh, yeah? I thought you wanted my opinion because I'm a genius."

Misty was silent. She sat hunched on the park bench looking lost. Stanley put a fatherly arm around her.

"Come on, Misto. Everything's going to be all right," he said. "Come on. Let's go to one of those grimy restaurants and eat hamburgers."

In the weeks they had been back together, Holly had mentioned someone named Arnold Milgrim several times. She neither explained nor described him, which led Guido to suspect that he was an established fact of Holly's life—for example, a current or former lover. But when Holly began to refer to him with a certain reverence in her voice, Guido imagined that Arnold Milgrim was someone universally known and respected, and not Holly's lover after all.

One morning, he could endure it no longer. He looked menacingly at Holly and menacingly at the coffeepot.

"Pour me some of that Arnold Milgrim," he said.

Holly then explained that Arnold Milgrim had been a student of her grandfather's and that she had met him on her recent trip to France. He taught philosophy at Oxford on loan from Yale and was the author of *The Decay of Language as Meaning*, *The Automatic Memory*, and *Fishing in the Waters of Time*, which was about Marxist literature.

As the day progressed, it seemed to Guido that he was the sole citizen of New York who had not heard of Arnold Milgrim. Vincent had seen Arnold Milgrim on television in England. Stanley had once read *The Automatic Memory*. Finally, Guido broke down and called Misty, who said that she had read *The Decay of Language as Meaning* and found it provocative, but basically silly.

Then the subject was dropped. Guido persuaded Holly not to move, but to redecorate. The artifacts of stasis were to be dispelled by a series of painters, plasterers, and paperhangers who were scheduled to invade the apartment. In the evening, Guido was presented with large numbers of paint, fabric, and wallpaper samples. He and Holly sat at the dining room table planning, making sketches, and matching one color with another, or else they repaired to whichever room was the subject at hand and shoved furniture around.

After this collaborative effort, they lived under drop cloths for several weeks. Holly directed her attention to the workmen whom she bullied, cajoled, flattered, and flirted with. She made them pots of coffee and Italian sandwiches. As a result, not so much as a spot of paint marred the floors. The paperhangers were put into a state of awe and terror at the sight of her. The plasterer vacuumed up at the end of each day's work. Guido realized that his wife would have made an extremely efficient dictator.

Soft coats of unnecessary white paint were spread on the walls, except for the dining room, which at Guido's suggestion was pale apple green with white trim. Four Peruvians appeared to scrape, stain, and wax the floors. The Persian rugs came back from the cleaners. Two boys who looked a little like Stanley showed up and fixed the kitchen by building an ingenious counter and putting up some chic and useful shelves.

Finally, the last drop cloth was taken up. The rooms no longer smelled of paint and the curtains swung immaculately in the cold breeze.

One Saturday morning, the mail contained a heavy, cream-colored envelope addressed to Holly. It looked like a wedding invitation, but it was a letter from Arnold Milgrim announcing that he was coming to New York with one of his students. Holly immediately fired off a reply, inviting Arnold and his student for dinner.

Guido examined the envelope. It was embossed with the seal of Arnold Milgrim's college.

"Terrific paper," he said. "We should have done the hallway in it. Spear me another of those Arnold Milgrims." Holly absently dropped on his uplifted plate an Irish sausage.

Arnold Milgrim appeared on a Tuesday evening with his student, a girl whose toast-colored hair was so tenuously arranged that Guido was afraid to shake hands with her. Her name was Doria Mathers.

Arnold Milgrim was a small, muscular man. His suit looked as if it had been reduced to scale to fit a box turtle. He wore small, polished loafers and socks that were the deep red of arterial blood. He was bald and his face had the naked, political sensuality seen on the busts of Roman generals.

Doria Mathers was taller by a head and she looked extremely sleepy. She wore a long plum-colored dress and stockings that matched Arnold's socks. Both she and Arnold wore round, pink glasses.

By the time drinks were finished, Arnold had given Guido a chapter of his new book for *Runnymeade*. Doria, on the other hand, had hardly spoken. She did not raise her eyes from the sight of her own knees, but she was hardly a quiet presence. Later she said: "I fill my own space with a kind of inaudible loudness."

Guido sat next to her in front of the fireplace, filling her glass from time to time and wondering if a new form of communication had been invented without his knowing about it. On the other side of the room, Arnold chatted energetically to Holly.

"Doria is my most extraordinary student. She's American, you know. American universities didn't seem able to hold her. The sheer power of her mind oppresses her. In another age, she would have been a mystic, but in our mercantile era she is merely a genius. I have never seen anyone so overwhelmed by internal intelligence."

Holly looked over at Doria, who was silently communing with Guido. Something indeed seemed to have overwhelmed her—she could barely lift her head. At dinner, Doria uttered one complete sentence. She said: "I feel that jet lag is the disease most appropriate to the second half of the twentieth century."

That said, she bent her head and took tiny bites of

her quiche Lorraine, the dish Holly felt was correct to serve to people who have been on transatlantic flights.

As the evening wore on, Doria began to unravel. She took off her shoes, which lay one on top of the other under the coffee table. Her tenuous hair arrangement had begun to dissolve and hung sagging but stylish at the back of her neck. Her dress, which was more like an extremely long sweater, pulled to one side, revealing her white shoulder. Holly, whose neatness was like the sheen on an Oriental pearl, could see that there was quite a lot to be said for dishevelment.

Doria curled up in the corner of the couch and took from her carpet bag a ball of mouse-colored yarn and a pair of knitting needles. As the conversation continued around her, she stared at a point midway between Holly and Arnold Milgrim and knit mechanically.

On the sofa, Arnold was again enlightening Holly on the subject of Doria.

"She is completely interior. Apparently, she always has been. She didn't speak until she was four. It turned out she did in fact speak, but not in front of anyone. She had invented her own language, which she spoke to her toys. She still remembers it and has written a dictionary for it. She kept a diary in code. The key is in a safe deposit box. She isn't really shy, you know. She's just dreamlike and still. She worries constantly about overstimulation. It'll take her at least a week to take in this dinner party. When she first got to Oxford, she stayed in her room for a month just to absorb her immediate surroundings."

Then he asked Holly if she would show Doria around New York while Arnold went off to see his publisher.

"Will she be able to stand it?" Holly said.

"She has developed an intentional delayed reaction

facility," said Arnold. "When we get back to Oxford, she'll have to withdraw for a while."

As they left, Holly asked Doria what she might like to see.

"I'd like to go to all the knitting shops," Doria said. "I want to see some rustic, hand-pulled yarn. I would also like to see some colonial fabrics, and, if possible, I would like to have some contact with a loom."

Life was back to normal, sort of. Holly said: "Why is Vincent unavailable every time I ask him for dinner? I've seen him once since I've been back, and that's not enough. I want to check out this girl of his I've been hearing so much about. Is he actually spending every minute of his day with her?"

"Our Vincent is finally part of a pair," said Guido.

"Is that good news?" Holly said.

"It looks that way."

"Is he afraid to submit her to my scrutiny, or is he ashamed of me?" said Holly.

"I think it has to do with her, not him," said Guido. "She's what you might call a difficult case, but not in the way of his previous girls."

"That sounds very encouraging," Holly said. "Let's get them over here. You invite them. If I do, Vincent will think I'm snooping."

"You are snooping," said Guido. "Poor Vincent."

"Poor me," said Holly. "Vincent doesn't approve of me anymore. I don't think he'll ever forgive me for going away for a few weeks. Sometimes I think you won't either. But it was the best thing to do. I feel that a great many emotional cobwebs have been swept away."

Guido looked from his beautiful wife to his beautiful apartment. He did not remember ever seeing so much as a speck of dust, let alone a cobweb. But somewhere along the line, Holly was right. Their daily routine had always been extremely pleasing. Now it seemed magnificent. The real breakfast Holly believed in was more like a gift than a meal. As always, she read him items from the paper that she found entertaining, usually dim quotes from public officials, or equally dim remarks made by society matrons. These recitations, which Guido had always found charming, now seemed endearing. Her daily telephone call to his office made him gladder than ever. The walks they took, the dinners they had out, and the meals they had at home were no longer pleasant spots in the day, but events that brought them closer together. Holly's absence had put a sheen on her return. Their normal pastimes were not so normal now. It was undeniable that her trip to France had made life richer. Their evenings were rhapsodic and passionate. Their mornings were sweet and affectionate. Through all of this, Holly conducted herself like a bird of paradise that had flown through the window of a house in Des Moines and settled down; she explained very little. She let her presence be enjoyed. Guido's great happiness in her presence canceled out his bafflement when he was alone.

They ceased to discuss their separation, if separation it had been. What was the use of discussion? Holly simply went her own way, and if her way was not Guido's, Guido reminded himself that he was not married to his double. And now that she was back, he was happy. It was only when Holly went out that Guido realized how much her going away had hurt him. He knew it would wear off, but when Holly came back from so little as a trip around the corner to buy a bunch of parsley, Guido felt his life had been saved.

The idea of dinner with Guido and Holly appalled Misty.

"I will not sit around making nervous small talk over some garbagy rack of lamb," she said.

"You're not getting rack of lamb," said Vincent. "You're probably getting roast chicken. And there will be no nervous small talk. There will be calm, large-scale talk. Holly is very hot to meet you."

"I will not be observed," shouted Misty. "I will not be surveyed to see if I pass muster or if they think I'm good enough for you."

"Oh, Misty," Vincent said. "They'll think you're far too good for me. Guido likes you. I love you. How could you possibly not pass muster?"

"That's an egocentric notion if I ever heard one," Misty said. "I'm not going."

"I don't ask for much," said Vincent. "Jesus, it's only dinner. Guido is my oldest friend." He looked woebegone and puzzled.

This interchange took place in Misty's kitchen, where Vincent had been drying the dishes and feeling like a real adult. He put the dish towel down and discovered that Misty had stomped off into the living room and was standing by the window. It had begun to snow. Vincent stood beside her and gently turned her toward him. To his amazement, he saw that her eyes were filled with tears. His heart failed.

"Misty, what is it? It's only dinner." To his further astonishment, she put her head on his chest and wept onto his shirt.

It was the first time Vincent had ever seen her cry. She never cried, not even in the movies. Vincent suspected that she cried in private, but this, of course, was public. She had never even snuffled. He was filled with awe and panic.

"Do you know how much I love you?" he whispered into her hair.

"If you love me so much, give me a handkerchief."

He looked steadily at her. Her cheeks were wet, but her eyes were clear.

"How can you be this way, Misty? How can you be so flip when I'm serious?"

"You get mushy only when I cry," said Misty.

"I'm always mushy," said Vincent. "And I've never seen you cry before." He handed her his handkerchief.

"Misty," he said. "Do you have any feelings for me at all?"

"Enough," she said. "More than you deserve." Then she pressed her head against the window and began to cry again. He took her into his arms and begged her to explain.

"What the hell am I supposed to wear?" she sobbed. "Oh, God, this is awful."

Vincent took the handkerchief from her hand and gently dried her tears. He asked her to marry him. She told him that he was asking because she had broken down, and then she suggested a game of gin.

"If I win, will you marry me?" Vincent asked. He shuffled the cards with professional aplomb.

"How can you be so flip when I'm serious?" said Misty, and ginned out after four picks.

The next day, Misty paced around her office like a caged cat. At lunchtime she went out and bought a silk blouse she could not afford and a box of marrons glacés she also could not afford. The marrons were to be taken to Guido and Holly, but they were secretly for Vincent, who adored them. She slunk through a couple of shops, gazed in store windows, and thought of calling Maria Teresa to see if she wanted to come out and have a sandwich. It would be calming to talk to someone, but what was left to say? Instead, Misty talked silently to herself.

It was all over, she thought. What was all over was the person she had been all her life until yesterday—a person on the verge of something. She had been that person for so long it frightened her to give it up. That person had been waiting for The Big Event. The Big Event, of course, was love. Love had to do with flexing your personality to see what it might attract. What it attracted was some resplendent being who dropped from the sky and immediately loved you for your character. That the resplendent figure was Vincent Cardworthy seemed somewhat unbelievable to Misty, but there it was. He had dropped out of the sky and he loved her for her character.

She could put him off no longer. She had put him off to give herself the leisure to make up her mind about him. That was the intelligent woman's way to gauge love. But of course she hadn't put Vincent off at all, she realized. She had put herself off. Vincent accused her of nastiness, but she knew that if she expressed even a small amount of the tenderness she felt she would be in tears most of the time.

Now, as she walked slowly back to her office, the world looked askew. Nothing seemed to fit. Intelligence had nothing to do with this at all. The jig was up. She was in love.

Vincent came to claim her at five o'clock.

"Do we have time to go home before we go to Guido and Holly's?" Misty said.

Vincent nodded.

She sat in the taxi looking like a child being dragged off to the dentist. When they got to her apartment, she took a nap on the couch. Vincent stared at her from behind the newspaper. Even in sleep she looked intelligent. Vincent went back to his paper. The sight of Misty asleep always affected him. It made him feel woolly and tender.

Misty woke abruptly and felt awful. She groped around for her glasses, couldn't find them, and sat very still, looking unfocused and bereft, as if she had awakened from a kind dream to find merciless and cruel reality waiting for her. Vincent thought he understood unhappiness, but he was not sure if this was it. He sat beside her and took her hand.

"Are you going to tell me what's going on?" he said. "I can't bear to see you this way."

She shrugged her shoulders.

Vincent asked, "Does it help if I tell you I love you, or does it make it worse?"

She began to cry. It was the second time in two days, but its effect on Vincent was not dimmed by repetition.

"Okay," she said. "Here goes."

His heart seemed to stop. This was it, but what was it?

"It's not what you're thinking," said Misty, looking at his stricken face. "It's worse. You're stuck with me. This is your last chance to bail out, Vincent. I don't think we were made for each other. Maybe you were made for me, but I was made for Attila the Hun."

"Are you telling me that life with you will be a living hell?"

"I am giving you one last chance to go off and find some nicer girl," said Misty. "Someone who knows her way around a sailboat."

"That's a disgusting thing to say. Last week you gave me a very compelling analysis on the workings of my stunning intellect. Now I'm supposed to take my intellect off and go sailing?"

"And besides that, there's the Jewish question," said Misty.

"Oh, that," said Vincent. "I don't notice either of us being religious. Besides, my Aunt Marcia is Jewish. She married Uncle Walter. She's everybody's favorite relative. What's the big deal?"

"Our backgrounds are very different," said Misty.

"This is not worth discussing," said Vincent. "We've done very well up till now, and we'll continue to do well."

"I'm not like your other flames," said Misty. "I don't know anything about dog breeding."

"Yes, you do," said Vincent. "The night we were comparing eccentric relatives, you told me that your Aunt Harriet wanted to cross Welsh corgis and Doberman pinschers and get a vicious but barkless guard dog for sneak attacks. That will be quite sufficient. Throw in my Aunt Marcia and you can see that we are ideally suited."

Tears slid out of the corners of Misty's eyes. She put her arms around his neck.

"I'm just scared," she said. "That's all."

"That isn't all," said Vincent. "What are you scared of?"

"I don't know."

"What else don't you know?"

"That's all," said Misty.

"I assume that means that you have given a good deal of analytical thought to your feelings about me."

"My feelings about you appear to transcend analysis."

"Wonderful," said Vincent. "What are they?"

"I just love you," she mumbled.

"Speak up, please," said Vincent.

"I said, I just love you. Isn't that banal?"

"What a relief," said Vincent, smiling.

With the box of marrons glacés under Misty's arm and a small bunch of sweetheart roses in Vincent's fist, they walked down the hallway to Holly and Guido. Before he rang their bell, Vincent backed Misty up against the wall and kissed her.

"You're crushing the marrons," she said.

"I don't care," said Vincent. "Half an hour ago you said that you would marry me."

"Only because you got down on your knee in the middle of the street and I was afraid you would be run over by a taxi."

"Can we announce it?" Vincent said.

"That you were almost run over?"

"That we're getting married. Kindly give me a yes or no answer. I can't take any more elegant defense."

"Yes," said Misty.

"It'll be nice—all of us together," said Vincent.

"Aren't you the happy Boy Scout," said Misty.

The table was set for four. The coffee was put out for six.

"Arnold Milgrim and his student are coming for coffee," said Guido.

"It may be that only Arnold is coming," said Holly. "Doria seems to have disappeared with Misty's cousin."

"Stanley?" said Misty.

"Stanley," said Guido. "Arnold and Doria came to the office this afternoon. Arnold and I closeted ourselves in my office to go over the article he's giving to *Runnymeade* and when we emerged, they had vanished."

"Amazing," said Misty. "Who on earth would run off with Stanley?"

The evening was easier than Misty had anticipated. At the door, there had been affection all around. Vincent and Guido clasped each other. Vincent kissed Holly. Guido kissed Misty. Holly and Misty shook hands and gave each other the thrice over. It didn't much matter to Misty whether or not she liked Holly. She was bound to like Holly whether she liked her or not, since Holly was about to become a fact of Misty's life. Holly treated Misty as if she had known her for years. Then she shepherded Misty into the kitchen.

"I just wanted to get you under the light," said Holly.

Misty stood obligingly and displayed full face, three-quarters, and profile.

"Excellent," said Holly. "Even better than I thought. I wouldn't have given Vincent credit for this much sense. My theory is that Vincent has just awakened from an altered state of consciousness to find you. Get the champagne out of the fridge, will you?"

On the way to the dinner table, Vincent made his announcement.

"Misty and I have decided to get married," he said. This engendered another spate of handshakes, and kisses all around.

They drank a great deal of wine at dinner. Misty felt the candlelight reflecting in her eyes as she looked around the table. Everyone at the table looked beautiful and kind to her. Holly behaved as if she had simply incorporated Misty, but Guido seemed quite moved. There are going to be thousands of dinners like this, thought Misty. This is my place at the dinner table. This is my intended husband's best friend and that is the wife of my intended's best friend whom I am going to spend the rest of my life getting to know. Across the table, Vincent looked seraphically happy. How wonderful everything tasted, Misty thought. Everything had a sheen on it. Was that what

131

love did, or was it merely the wine? She decided that it was love.

It was just as she suspected: love turned you into perfect mush.

After dinner, Arnold Milgrim and Doria Mathers appeared. Doria looked more windblown than ever.

"This is a flying visit," said Arnold. "Just a cup of coffee and we must dash."

Holly did the introductions.

"Stanley has the same last name as you," said Doria to Misty. "Is that common in New York, or are you kin?"

"First cousins," said Misty.

"Blood relatives," said Doria. "How thick. The idea of cousinship has lost its meaning in the modern world. It is entirely volitional, I feel. For example, I have several cousins. A few of them I have never seen. Some of them I remember hating and I have actually forgotten the names of two or three of them. Water, in the sense of distances, is now far thicker than blood, I feel. Your cousin reads Greek divinely. He read Plato to me this afternoon."

No one had any reply to this statement. Holly poured the coffee and sat next to Arnold. On the other side of the room Vincent, Misty, and Guido clustered around Doria, who, Misty noticed, although not a small girl, had a knack of making ordinary objects seem tiny in her hands. She huddled over her coffee cup, which she held with both hands, as if it were a bird's egg. It was impossible to make conversation in her vicinity, but even in a silent group, with Doria as the focus, one felt that quite a lot was going on somewhere.

"Doria engenders thought," said Arnold confidentially to Holly. "For example, the mechanics of emotional politics. Doria can inflict hurt, which she defines as power. I am quite sure that she and that Stanley went somewhere and quite innocently read Plato. But Doria knows that gesture sets off the idea of possibility."

This sounded to Holly very much like a statement of jealousy.

"The danger of communion between the sexes is that one falls back on the stereotypic," said Arnold. "By this I mean such pseudo-values as possessiveness. Or the idea of love as capitalism: return on investment. The very *idea* of Doria blitzes these conceptions. A mind like that must be shared in the way of a scientific discovery."

During this recitation, Arnold's eyes never left the couch on which Doria was sitting. Her head was bent as if her hair was weighting her down. She appeared to be asleep, but then she always appeared to be asleep.

"I must take her home," said Arnold. "She is on the point of frazzlement." He looked quite frazzled himself.

He got up and stood next to Doria, who gave him a glazed look. Then she drank her coffee the way a child gulps down milk, and Arnold took her home.

"Alone at last," said Guido. "Thank God the Quaker meeting is over. Let's have another bottle of champagne." They trooped back to the dining room.

"I drink to Misty and Vincent," said Guido.

"I drink to a lavish wedding," said Holly.

"No lavish weddings," said Misty. "You know what they say: the elaborateness of the wedding is in inverse proportion to the duration of the marriage."

"Who says that?" Vincent asked.

"I say it," said Misty.

"Does that mean you want to be married to me forever?" said Vincent.

"I'm marrying you, aren't I?"

Guido poured more champagne.

"Misty thinks all this institutionalizing of love makes you live outside the moral universe," said Vincent.

"I drink to the moral universe," said Guido.

They clicked their glasses and drank happily to the moral universe in the flickering light of Holly's beeswax candles.

CHAPTER 6

MISTY AND VINCENT STAGGERED HOME AND into bed. The champagne was wearing off.

"Well, now it's official," said Vincent. "Are you having second thoughts?"

"I never have second thoughts," said Misty. "It's against my religion to have second thoughts or to enter the city of Mecca. Are you?"

"I'd express my deep joy to you," said Vincent, "but unfortunately I can't seem to get any of my limbs to work."

At breakfast, Vincent had difficulty moving his head.

"I'd be the happiest man in the United States if I didn't have such an enormous headache," he said.

Misty, however, was back to normal. Having carried her love around like an albatross, she felt as well placed in the world as a fresh loaf of bread.

"You should be sick as a dog," said Vincent. "I don't understand it. You never drink, whereas I am a man of the world. Therefore, you should be hung over and not me. Am I shouting?"

Misty set a glass of orange juice before him.

"That juice is very bright," he said. "Do you think I could have some coffee first?"

Misty brought him his cup, with which he saluted her.

"Here's to our happy future," he said.

"Your optimism is truly record-breaking," said Misty.

"What's wrong with happy futures?"

"This is the twentieth century," said Misty. "Not hardly the great age of happy futures."

"There are happy futures for some," he said.

"You and your debutante fantasies," said Misty.

Holly had arranged to meet Doria Mathers at a tea-room. She had spent the morning perusing the telephone book trying to find a loom to get Doria into contact with. Her research revealed that knitting was a very popular indoor sport and that a loom was on permanent display at the Wool Institute, which also had a few samples of colonial fabric.

She was not much looking forward to this lunch: Holly liked her geniuses verbal; Doria, that interior wizard, was obviously capable of a silent meal. Holly did not approve of silent meals. She believed in dinner-table conversation and one of the things she loved about Guido was that he was a first-rate dining companion.

Doria, however, turned up talkative. The flip-side of interior silence seemed to be exterior gabbiness. Doria took tiny bites of her sandwich in between which she went on at some length about Arnold Milgrim. She said he was the greatest man she had ever met, and possibly the greatest man who had ever lived. It turned out that she and Arnold were going to be married, even though Arnold, who had been married once before, did not believe that exalted love needed social trappings.

"There are people I have met . . ." said Doria, lowering her voice to a whisper, "who centuries ago would have been proclaimed saints. Isn't it interesting that only the church has saints? The world has only merit, which is not sufficient. These people are saints of the mind. Their sacrifice is the sacrifice to the intellect. We need a new definition of holiness for times in which religion isn't relevant. Arnold is on the path to that sort of sanctity, I feel. He is all man, all mind. I, on the other hand, am entirely temperament. For example, I feel I must have two ounces of chocolate every day. Arnold has no quirks of that sort. He has no specific needs at all. He is beyond temperament and personality. He is simply spirit, motivated by ideas. I am a case of entrenched but suspended personality. Arnold says I am capable of profound and unexpected petulance as well as its transcendence."

Doria was wearing an angora dress that had stretched in some places and shrunk in others. The heel on one of her shoes looked on the point of breaking. To ward off the cold, she wore as a cape what looked like a series of horse blankets with exposed seams. In the yarn shops, she did business briskly. Otherwise, she was a study in manifest chaos.

Holly was impeccable. She had not opted for neatness: it had been thrust upon her by nature. Her thick hair was always precisely cut and her unadorned features gave her an air of calm. Clothes looked neater and cleaner and more starched on her than they did on others. Hours of stalking yarn did not disarrange her in any way, while Doria looked almost frenzied. Holly watched as her piled hair slipped slowly down her neck. At the Wool Institute, her cape began to slide. Holly was transfixed. It had not occurred to her before that sloppiness might be a calculated style. Clearly, Doria was on to something. She stood in charming dishevelment in front of the Institute's loom.

"I feel that weaving is a precise metaphor for the way in which life is made," she said. "By which I mean individually constructed. Any strand can be woven in at the dictation of the imagination. I think of the philosophy of history as a loom of that sort. It is, isn't it?"

"Quite," said Holly.

Holly dropped her off at the hotel. Doria had bought hand-pulled yarn from Vermont, raw wool from Pakistan, tapestry yarn, twisted sock thread from the Himalayas, and a skein of alpaca. She shook Holly's hand goodbye.

"I'm very tired now," she said. "Arnold and I are flying back to England. Thank you for all your input."

That night over dinner, Holly asked Guido if he thought she was capable of profound and unexpected petulance and its transcendence.

"No," said Guido. "I think you are capable of superficial and completely thought-out petulance."

"Arnold *formulates* about Doria," said Holly. "Do you ever formulate about me?"

"I try not to," said Guido. "As for Doria, I think she's either drunk or drugged or extremely silly."

"I think they're very romantic," said Holly.

Over the peach mousse, Holly said, "I often think our temperaments are at variance."

Guido threw down his spoon.

"Goddamn it, Holly. You go off and leave me and then can't get out a coherent sentence as to why. You come back and don't explain yourself. Then you want

138

me to formulate about you. And you think that Milgrim and his sloppy girlfriend are romantic. The only thing profound about you is your constant wrongheadedness."

With that, he stormed into the living room and brooded. He rarely lost his temper. To him it was like losing his keys. But as he sat in his armchair, he realized how sweet righteous anger really was.

He looked up to find Holly standing meekly in the doorway, carrying coffee cups on a tray.

"I'm sorry," she said. "Sometimes everything is so smooth and invisible that I can't see it without discord."

Guido sat without speaking.

"You're the only person I've ever loved," said Holly.

"Good," said Guido. "Glad to hear it. Since you love me so, do you ever formulate about me?"

"Of course not," said Holly. "I don't think that way. You do. I simply love you."

He gave her a look of love and grief.

"Whatever," he said. "You are frequent hell to live with."

Misty walked slowly past the Museum of Natural History. Her heart at the moment had four chambers, filled with love, dread, confusion, and certainty.

She was getting married. The thought of it astounded her. This great leap forward made her feel like her own shadow. When other girls got married, they were filled with joy, not rumination. Each event in the walk toward marriage was supposed to be taken with untainted gladness—wasn't it?

The truth was that Misty had never given the notion of marriage any thought at all. Now, she was infusing it with all manner of sentimentality. This, she felt, was the price you paid for never envisioning your father walking you down the aisle, or a little cottage by the sea, or a honeymoon spent touring the château district or bicycling in Bermuda.

She had never thought about the mechanics of marriage: she had thought only about love. The mechanics, however, were there to be dealt with. These preyed on her mind and made her grim, but they expanded Vincent's boundless optimism: all life was an adventure. All events contributed to the gaiety of nations. All people were flowers embroidered on the rich, entertaining tapestry of life.

Misty was thinking about family. She and Vincent had broken the news to their respective sets of parents and soon their families would be united. Vincent found this a charming prospect and thought about it very little. Misty faced this with alarm and thought about it constantly.

Vincent's parents lived in the small town of Petrie, Connecticut. The family had lived in and around Midland County since the beginning of time, it seemed. Life, for the Cardworthys, was patterned. The family had helped found the Petrie Country Day School and all members of the family were sent to it. The women of the family were community pillars. They ran the library subscription, the garden club, the Petrie Lecture Society, the Midland County Improvement and Preservation Society, and the annual hospital art show. Once in a while, a Cardworthy ran for local office and was elected. One of these Cardworthys had served in the state senate and had eventually gone to Washington. Mostly they were country lawyers or country doctors. Vincent's father was a lawyer. His mother was an Edith Whartonite and a fanatic gardener. The only eccentric in the family was Aunt Lila, who had bred the rose named after her cleaning lady. Now she was working on another she intended to name after the man who serviced her car.

Vincent's family was tranquil. Misty's family, on the other hand, was far too exciting. Her family included Communists, Trotskyists, socialists of every stripe, union organizers, professors of political science, neurophysiologists, and lay analysts.

Misty's great-grandfather had come from Russia with his brother, who was a tin broker. In the United States, they did not settle in a large urban center but went west as tin peddlers and smiths. In Chicago they accrued a little capital with which they repaired to the town of Medicine Stone, Wisconsin. There Misty's great-grandfather bought a dairy farm and his brother opened a dry goods store. Misty's father and her uncle Bernie were grandsons of the pioneers. Uncle Bernie said that when he wrote his autobiography he would call it *Jew Boy of the Prairie*. Berkowitz cousins still ran the dairy farm and the dry goods store. Misty's father had been sent to Chicago to be educated and had stayed there. He was a labor lawyer. Uncle Bernie had gone to Chicago too, but Uncle Bernie was a crook.

The family put its communal hand over its communal heart when Uncle Bernie's name was mentioned. No one was sure what his crime had been or if, in fact, there had been any crime. But after a career as a song plugger, Uncle Bernie had done something funny in the sheet music business and had absconded with a large sum of money to the Bahamas. He came back to the States only to see his lawyers. Uncle Bernie had also written a song that had had a brief vogue in the forties when it had been recorded by Dan Staniels's Gopher Band. The song was called "Dancing Chicken" and it celebrated the courtship rites of Prout's Hen, a cousin to Attwater's Prairie Chicken, whose rituals

141

Uncle Bernie had observed as a young boy. This is what Vincent's family had in store.

"I can't marry you," Misty said to Vincent. "My family is too weird."

"Your father is a lawyer and Stanley's father is a professor," said Vincent. "That seems very dull to me."

"That's only two out of many," said Misty.

"Not to worry," said Vincent. "Wait until you meet my cousin Hester."

Misty did not want to meet Vincent's cousin Hester or any other family member. The whole idea of family meetings, weddings, apartment searches put her off. What did any of this have to do with love, anyway?

The subject of family kept cropping up. It sprouted one evening during a dinner with Stanley and Sybel Klinger. They were sitting on the floor of a restaurant called the True Life Inn, one of the few eating places in New York that served what Sybel thought was food.

Vincent poked his chopsticks into a large bowl of vegetables and pulled out something punctured with holes.

"Do you eat this?" he said. "Or did it fall off someone's shoe?"

"That's lotus root," said Sybel.

"And what's this stuff that looks like green hair?"

"That's seaweed," said Sybel primly. "It purifies your body and puts minerals in. There are certain tribes of Indians that live on it and they never get any blood diseases."

"Don't ask what it is," said Stanley. "Just chow it down. It's great for you, man. So you guys are getting married. That's really far out. Did you tell everyone yet? I mean family."

"It's entirely official now," said Vincent.

"That's really something," said Stanley. "Wait till you meet all of us. Wait till you meet my brother Michael. but we don't call him Michael. We all call him Muggs. He married this girl named Nancy and we all call her Ninny. Muggs and Ninny."

"What do Muggs and Ninny do?" Vincent asked.

"Well, Ninny teaches children how to be more artistically aware," said Stanley. "And Muggs is carrying on the great Berkowitz song-writing tradition. Did you tell Vincent about Muggs's opera?"

"No." said Misty.

"What opera?" said Vincent.

"Muggs wrote this opera," said Stanley. "It's called *Thirteen in Miami*. It's about how the apocalypse takes place during this lavish bar mitzvah at the Fontainebleau Hotel, but no one will produce it because they all think it's too strange. So Muggs writes movie music and makes a lot of dough."

Misty sighed. Getting married changed everything. Here she was sitting on the floor eating out of a communal pot with her husband-to-be, her cousin, and her cousin's girlfriend. This was the sort of evening you preserved in amber, against your will, and found it years later as a pre-nuptial memory. Perhaps she would remember it with fondness Perhaps she would remember Sybel as adorable. Perhaps she would remember herself as adorable. How she hated it all. What she wanted to do was to go down to City Hall and get it over with. She stared glumly at her plate. Sybel was giving them a lecture on nutrition.

"You can kill your cells with bad food," she said. "People won't face the fact that the way they eat is just like suicide only slower. Another thing is that your spine is the center of your energy and what you eat goes directly into your spine. If anything happens to your spine, that's it. This masseur I go to can tell everything that's wrong with you from your spine. I mean, he told me that I had a potassium deficiency and he was right. He could tell just from my back. This dancer I knew had stomach trouble only he didn't know he did and this masseur diagnosed it. I mean, if you eat wrong, your spine starts to atrophy. People think neurosis is in your mind but it's in your spine."

Misty uttered a silent prayer that Stanley would never marry Sybel or anyone like her. Finally, they finished their mint tea, Sybel finished her lecture, and it was time to go home.

Sybel and Stanley walked ahead. Misty and Vincent strolled some distance behind.

"Is Sybel a runaway slave?" said Vincent. "Or is there something wrong with her feet? She seemed to have some sort of shackles on her ankles."

"Those are her leg weights," said Misty. "She says they keep her calf muscles clear and full of physical intelligence."

"She ought to try wrapping one around her head," said Vincent.

"Vincent," said Misty, "can we go to City Hall to get married? Just the two of us? Can't we elope?"

"Are you ashamed of marrying me in public?" said Vincent.

"We can have a reception afterward. Please, Vincent, if we're going to do it, let's just do it."

"Okay," said Vincent. "It's nice to know you want it done. Of course, this will break our mothers' hearts. My father called today and told me that no time has been wasted. Your mother wrote my mother and my mother wrote your mother and their letters crossed. Now they've been on the telephone cooing to each other. They've dug up this ecumenical team— a rabbi and minister act who are all set to go."

"I can't stand this," said Misty. "I will not have

144

drippy relatives talking to me about mixed marriages. I want to get a blood test, a license, and get married."

"Think of the presents we won't get," said Vincent.

"Don't you worry," said Misty fiercely. "We'll get."

That night, they made a few decisions. Misty's apartment was well equipped but small. Vincent's was bare, but large. He also had furniture in storage, left to him by a childless great uncle. Therefore it was decided that Vincent's apartment would be painted and that they would move into it. Misty's lease was almost up, which Vincent took as providential.

The next day, she began to pack her books, arrange her clothes, and get estimates from moving companies.

That evening, after dinner, they went to Vincent's to get the lay of the land. His kitchen, which had been used only to boil water in, was bigger than Misty's. The living room looked out over the tops of the London plane trees on the street. There was a big bedroom and a small, empty room that looked perfect for a double study. Vincent had two large closets. One was filled with clothes. The other was filled with junk.

From this closet he removed a large steamer trunk and began to unpack it. Inside there was a Santa Claus costume; a soccer trophy; crumpled diplomas from the Petrie Country Day School and its kindergarten; a Boy Scout banner and a good citizen award on a scroll; a needlepoint tennis racket cover that bore a portrait of Alex, the Cardworthy terrier who had died when Vincent was fifteen; a copy of a book entitled *Your Tropical Fish* by someone called Eugene Cardworthy, who was not a relative; and an unopened pack of Hawaiian cigarettes. Vincent looked at the cigarettes with puzzlement.

145

"I've never been to Hawaii," he said. "I didn't know they made their own cigarettes. I wonder where I got them from. Don't smirk at that Santa Claus outfit. I was a Santa Claus for charity at college." He rummaged happily in the trunk. "Look at this!" He held up a blue T-shirt on whose front the words GARBAGE HERO had been stenciled.

"I hired myself out on a sanitation crew for two weeks when I was doing a time-motion study," he said. "The fellows made this up for me. One of them said: 'You think of us as garbage collectors, but we think of you as garbage producers.'"

"This is like living in a museum devoted to adolescence," said Misty.

Misty had almost no souvenirs. It took her three days to pack. The only thing she carried over by hand was her glass photograph and a bronze lamp she had bought in Paris that had two tulip-shaped glass shades. The people in the photograph were her ancestors—the Jewish homesteaders of Medicine Stone, Wisconsin.

Within a month, Vincent's apartment began to look less like a waiting room and more like a home. His furniture was out of storage and there was now an oak dining table with four chairs, a settee, a desk for the study, and a large painting of a sandhill crane to hang over the fireplace.

Vincent hung the glass photograph in the bedroom.

"Medicine Stone," said Vincent musingly. "What a wonderful name."

"It was immortalized in song by my Uncle Bernie," said Misty. "He wrote the song about Prout's Hen that Stanley told you about."

"Sing it," said Vincent.

"Okay," said Misty. "It's the Berkowitz family anthem, which as you know is called 'Dancing Chicken':

I've been to London, England
And I've been to Paris, France
Now I wanna go home
Back to Medicine Stone
And watch Prout's chicken dance.
I wanna watch them chickens dance
It's more like a strut but it means romance
Back to back, feather to feather
When Prout's chickens get together.

"Sing it again," said Vincent. "I have to memorize it. Is that Uncle Bernie's only song?"

"He wanted to write a follow-up about Attwater's Prairie Chicken, but he never got around to it."

A few days later, Vincent and Misty had blood tests and, much faster than Misty had anticipated, obtained a marriage license. They decided they wanted witnesses after all. Vincent would have Guido and Holly, and Misty would have Maria Teresa Warner and Stanley. Sybel was not allowed to come. The night before their excursion to City Hall, they were stricken with insomnia.

"My hands are cold and my feet are burning," said Vincent, throwing off the covers.

"I'm starving," said Misty.

"I don't understand that. We had a huge dinner."

"We didn't have dinner," said Misty.

"We didn't? I don't remember not having dinner."

"I don't feel very well," said Misty.

"I've lost my memory," said Vincent. "Let's get up and be nervous."

They stood in front of the refrigerator.

"You can have yogurt, bananas, or yogurt and bananas," said Misty. "Or you can have peanut butter and jelly or you can have a bunch of wilted watercress."

147

"I want spaghetti," said Vincent.

"It's half past two. You can't have spaghetti," said Misty.

"Oh, yes, I can," said Vincent. "It's my wedding night. I'm going to have spaghetti with butter and garlic. It's good luck to get married with indigestion."

"If you're going to make spaghetti," said Misty, "make enough for two. And you might have the decency to put on a robe. It's bad luck to face a pot of boiling water on your wedding night with no clothes on."

The bride wore a white wool suit and a green silk blouse. The suit was a relic of Paris, bought in a fit of longing to look like a chic Parisian. It had never been worn—Misty had been too frightened of spilling something on it.

The groom wore what he called his banker's suit with a sprig of freesia in his buttonhole. A twin sprig was pinned to the bride's lapel.

Out of pure sentimentality, Vincent had trooped to the Greek florist to get Misty a bouquet.

"Something for a horse?" said the florist.

"How did you remember all this time?" asked Vincent.

"I remember all the nuts in love," said the florist, wearily.

"Well, I'm getting married today," said Vincent. "In City Hall. I need a nice little bouquet of something."

"Same girl you got the horse blanket for?"

"Yes," said Vincent.

"Sure. Sure," said the florist, shrugging. "I give you a little bunch of lilies of the valley and throw in the freesia for nothing. Next time you'll be back after a fight. That's the way these things go."

The wedding party sat on hard chairs in City Hall, waiting to be called: Stanley, Guido, Vincent, Misty, and Maria Teresa Warner. Holly sat on the end eavesdropping on the conversations of the other couples.

A clerk appeared. "The Morosco party," he called. At this a group of ten stood up and filed into the magistrate's chambers. A few minutes later, the clerk reappeared.

"Gerkus and Bethnelson," he called. At this a man in cowboy boots, a red bandanna, and a checkered shirt stood up, holding the hand of a blond girl wearing orange trousers. Both carried large red carnations.

"Hold my hand," whispered Misty to Maria Teresa.

"Vincent's supposed to hold your hand, you dummy," said Maria Teresa.

"He's holding my other hand. I have to be anchored," said Misty. "Otherwise, I'm going to bolt. This is worse than waiting for an execution."

Maria Teresa held her hand. "You're supposed to be agitated," she said. "You're getting married."

Stanley stared straight ahead. He whispered to Guido that the shabby anteroom in which they sat looked rather like the detention hall in a high school. Even so, the solemnity of the occasion overwhelmed him. Holly sat impeccably in her chair.

"It's taking Gerkus and Bethnelson longer than it took the Morosco party," said Vincent nervously to Guido.

Holly leaned over. "Gerkus and Bethnelson wrote their own ceremony," she said. "I heard them arguing about who was going to say what. Bethnelson is the girl. Her name is Alice. His name is Fred. He was married once before. She wanted to get married on May Day. They're going to read from John Stuart Mill and a letter of Rosa Luxemburg's. They aren't going to obey, either."

"They don't have to," said Vincent. "This is a civil ceremony. It takes about five seconds."

The clerk appeared.

"The magistrate is having a cup of coffee," he said. "All that talking makes his throat dry. He'll be right with you folks. Cardworthy, right?"

"Right," said Vincent. Misty's hand was shaking in his, but Vincent believed himself to be steady. He was thinking about Holly and Guido's wedding on the lawn of Holly's grandmother's house in Moss Hill. A little girl had scattered rose petals. A little boy had brought the ring down the aisle on a blue satin pillow. Vincent felt in his pocket for his own ring. This was meant to be a surprise—Misty hadn't said anything about a ring. On the advice of Holly, Vincent had measured her finger while she was sleeping and with this information had bought what the jeweler said was a Victorian friendship ring—a gold circle whose thick gold strands formed a love knot.

Guido and Holly's was the only wedding he could remember. As he sat on the uncomfortable chair, he was glad he and Misty did not have to put up with any scattered petals or blue satin pillows. The shabby room, the shabby clerk, the nervous-looking wedding parties wearing street clothes seemed right to him. According to the plans he and Misty had made with their respective parents, they were to fly to Chicago for a party, and then travel to Petrie for another. That would be quite enough festivity, Vincent felt. He felt their love was quite rich enough to do without any ornamentation. He had mentioned this to Misty over coffee at breakfast. At this declaration, he noticed that there were tears in her eyes.

"Give me back my hand," said Maria Teresa. "I have something for you. I was going to give it to you afterward, but I'll give it to you now. Besides, your

150

hand's all steamy." She took from her handbag a flat package wrapped in pink paper and tied with a white ribbon. Misty opened it. Inside was a can of sardines with a card that read: "Anyone who gave me so much as a sardine could obtain anything from me."

"At midnight, you and Vincent have a sardine sandwich," said Maria Teresa.

"Cardworthy party," called the clerk. They all stood up and filed in. Guido was wearing a sober suit with a sprig of lily of the valley in his lapel. He was meditating on the generosity of friendship and on the feeling that one steps outside oneself in happiness for one's friends. As they stood in front of the magistrate, Guido saw the diamonds twinkling on Holly's ears. Vincent looked shy and serious. Misty was almost expressionless except for her eyes, which looked either stricken or full of tears. Guido felt someone grip his hand. It was Stanley, who had cut his hair short for the occasion and was wearing his three-piece suit. Everyone seemed to be connected to someone else. Maria Teresa stood clutching Holly's elbow. Misty and Vincent exchanged vows holding hands.

It had been raining when they started out. Through the high windows, Guido could see big, gray, early spring clouds. A shaft of weak light illuminated them all. When Vincent slipped the ring on Misty's finger, Guido felt that he might weep. He was very, very happy.

Vincent and Misty stood on the steps of City Hall. The state had pronounced them husband and wife, after which they had fled down the hall ahead of the others.

"How did you know what size ring to get?" said Misty.

"Holly told me to measure while you were asleep," said Vincent.

The April wind blew up around them. They heard the others clattering down the steps.

"Okay," yelled Stanley. "Look alive!" They turned and Stanley pelted them with a handful of rice.

"There's an ordinance against rice throwing," said Vincent. "Didn't you see the sign? Someone is going to slip down the steps and sue the city for millions of dollars."

"Aw, you gotta have rice at a wedding," said Stanley. "It's white rice too. Jesus, Sybel would kill me. This stuff has no nutritional value, she says. She says it's like eating straight poison. I had to slink into the store to get it."

"Let's go out to lunch," said Vincent. "After all, it's our wedding day."

"That's all been taken care of," said Holly. "Come with us."

Holly did not believe that marriage was valid without cake and she did not believe that vows were final without breakfast. For Vincent and Misty, she had pulled out all the stops. The wedding party sat around the dining room table while Guido poured the champagne. In the center of the table was a dish of orchids and white roses. The cloth was damask with big damask napkins. As they drank their champagne, Holly fed them scrambled eggs, kippers, sausages, and bacon.

"Now it's time for dessert," said Holly. "I thought Misty would hate one of those white cakes with those awful brides and grooms on the top."

"Gee," said Vincent. "I would have loved one of those white cakes with a bride and groom on the top. One of those grooms with painted shoes. I won't feel married until I get one of those grooms." Vincent was a little tipsy.

Holly brought out a platter on which towered a

pyramid of cream puffs stuck together with glazed sugar and dotted with Jordan almonds.

"A croquembouche," said Misty. "I never thought I'd have one of those for my very own."

"It's a French wedding cake," said Holly.

"It doesn't have little black feet," said Vincent. "You cut it, Misty; I'm too far gone."

"I wonder if anyone bothered to call the office," said Maria Teresa Warner. "I said I was home sick."

"I said I was getting married," said Vincent. "But no one except Shelly on the switchboard seemed to care."

"I forgot," said Misty.

"So did I," said Stanley. "Hey, Guido, I won't be in today."

The last crumbs had been swept away. The last glass of champagne and cup of coffee had been emptied. The wedding party sprawled in the living room, recuperating.

"It'll take me a week to detoxify," said Stanley. "Jesus, what a sugar rush. Sybel says that when you eat a lot of sugar, it shows up in your eyes."

"It's time to go home," said Vincent. "If my legs will work. What time is it?"

"It's seven-thirty," said Guido.

"It is?" Vincent said. "How did it get so late? Come on, Misty. Let's kiss everybody and get out of here."

They stood at the doorway, kissing everybody. The living room was dark. Everyone felt quite wiped out.

"Just like a real wedding," said Guido. "We're all exhausted and about to be hung over."

More heartfelt kisses were exchanged. Misty and Holly embraced.

Out on the street, Stanley and Maria Teresa walked together.

"I think I'm falling in love with you," said Stanley. "I think you're wonderful."

"That's nice," said Maria Teresa. "I'm old enough to have been your high school teacher. Besides, I live on sugar and white rice."

"Can I come and visit you sometime?" said Stanley.

"No," said Maria Teresa. "Go home and sleep it off. It'll help you detoxify."

"Aw, gee," said Stanley. "It's not a wedding unless you fall in love."

Finally, the bride and groom were left alone. They stood in the living room of their apartment.

"This is worse than a first date." said Vincent. "What is a newly wedded couple supposed to do after they've been living together for months?"

"I don't know," said Misty. "I think the bride is supposed to cry and the groom is supposed to read the paper. Or maybe it's the other way around. Why don't we open these presents?"

"What presents?"

"The ones you carried home in the shopping bags," said Misty.

"I carried shopping bags home?" said Vincent. "Married a few hours and my memory's gone all to hell."

From Holly and Guido were French coffee cups and a matching pot. From Maria Teresa besides the can of sardines, was an Irish linen tablecloth. From Sybel, via Stanley, was a book entitled *Good Nutrition in Marriage* and from Stanley, a copy of Ovid in Latin.

"That'll come in handy," said Vincent.

"I'm starving," said Misty. "Let's have Maria Teresa's sardines."

"I'm in love," said Vincent. "If I give you one of these sardines, does that mean there is nothing I can't obtain from you?"

"Yes," said Misty. "We're supposed to feed them to each other."

They ate sardines on toast and drank coffee out of their new cups. Misty flipped through Sybel's book.

"It says here that most failure of communication in marriage is a result of protein overload," she said.

"I want to make a speech," said Vincent. "Don't flinch. I make lovely speeches, as you know. Here's my speech. I am entirely happy. I am a prince. I have just gotten married and I am in love. Life is a banquet. Do you have anything to say to that?"

"Yes," said Misty dreamily. "I have married a sap."

CHAPTER 7

VINCENT AND MISTY SAT ON THE LIVING ROOM floor surrounded by boxes and wrapping paper. Their apartment was engulfed by wedding presents.

"It's like Christmas every day," said Vincent. "And look how much good exercise we're providing the postman."

They had been married for a month and a half. During this time, they had flown with Vincent's parents to Chicago and then flown back to New York with Misty's parents and Vincent's parents, who then drove them all up to Petrie.

The meeting of the families had been a great success.

"Oh, you of little faith," said Vincent. "Look at them, will you? Sitting around cooing to one another and not paying any attention to us unless it's to pop flashbulbs in our faces."

"I don't want to see another flashbulb, bottle of

champagne, or relative for the next five years," said Misty.

In Chicago, Adalaide Berkowitz took Dorothy Cardworthy to the Art Institute. Walter Cardworthy was taken to Fritz Berkowitz's club. In Petrie, Walter Cardworthy took Fritz Berkowitz to his weekly lunch at the Windhover Inn—this lunch included his law partner, the local doctor, and a retired state senator who now wrote mystery novels. Dorothy Cardworthy took Adalaide Berkowitz to the Horticultural Society lunch and to the Petrie Antique Fair. Through all this, Vincent and Misty fidgeted with boredom and longed to be at home alone.

No one took it amiss when Aunt Bobo Berkowitz, wife of the former Trotskyist Uncle Sim, gave Misty and Vincent a crude wooden idol that she claimed was a fertility god. She had gotten it in Africa.

"Visiting the Third World is so inspiring," said Aunt Bobo.

Aunt Lila Willet showed up in Petrie with an armload of Mrs. Iris Domato roses. Vincent's Aunt Marcia gave them a lavishly illustrated Passover Haggadah with a note that read: "It's nice to have another Jew in the family."

Finally, Vincent and Misty were allowed to go home while their parents made plans for their disposition during the major holidays.

"We can rotate Christmas and Thanksgiving," said Adalaide Berkowitz.

"Or we can all be together," said Dorothy Cardworthy.

On this note, Vincent and Misty fled. Now they were surrounded by the fruits of these journeys.

"Who's Connie Georgianos?" said Vincent, reading a card.

"Plumbers union," said Misty. "Daddy is their counsel. What did they send?"

"It looks like a glass pumpkin," said Vincent. "Does sending a wedding present to your lawyer's daughter amount to a kickback?"

"It's not a kickback when it's a glass cookie jar," said Misty. "Unless there are a great many large bills stuffed inside. Who are the Spaacks?"

"Those awful little people who drank too much at my parents' reception," said Vincent. "I bet they sent something awful."

"They did," said Misty. "It's a silver toast rack."

"Plated," said Vincent. "What a pair of creeps. This card says only four thirty-one. Who's four thirty-one?"

"Electricians," said Misty. "What did they send?"

"A toaster, naturally."

"How nice that will look lined up next to our other two toasters," said Misty.

As the afternoon progressed, the corners of the living room became stuffed with wrapping paper, excelsior, and tissue.

"Okay," said Vincent. "Here's what's on my side. A wooden salad bowl. A glass salad bowl. A pottery salad bowl. A martini shaker. A set of demitasse—no, two sets of demitasse, one red and white one with little flowers. A fake Russian icon from one of your Commie uncles, a cut-glass ashtray, and two silver serving spoons. What have you got?"

"Three tablecloths, a covered vegetable dish, a family of charlotte molds," Misty said, "an expresso pot, a covered basket, a silver toothpaste key, a carving knife, three silver candy dishes, a watercolor of a Cuban cane field from my other Commie uncle, and an unidentifiable object from some people called Aunt Betsy and Uncle Herbert. Who are they?"

"They weren't there. They're very small and elderly and live in Maine. Hand it over. Let's have a look."

The object in question was a carved wooden cylinder with a silver top.

"It's not a flask," said Vincent. "It isn't really a container. Is it an objet d'art?"

"Let's just put it on the shelf and forget it," said Misty. "I'm a little sick of all this stuff, aren't you?"

"No," said Vincent. "I am a materialist and I feel we deserve every bit of this because of the spiritual nature of our great love. And there's more to come. I have a whole list of people who haven't coughed up yet."

The two most prominent no-shows on Vincent's list were Misty's Uncle Bernie and Vincent's cousin Hester Gallinule, a former soap-opera actress now turned Broadway theater producer. They showed up, one after the other.

One evening, Misty came home to find Vincent deep in conversation with someone embedded in the wing chair. All she could see was the tip of a cigar. It was Uncle Bernie without a doubt. No one else's cigars smelled that good.

Uncle Bernie rose from his chair and engulfed his niece in a huge bear hug. He was a big man who wore a three-piece suit, a silk shirt, and a hand-painted tie. He and Vincent were chomping happily on Havana cigars and drinking whisky out of cut-glass tumblers sent by one of Vincent's distant relatives.

Uncle Bernie was huge. He had big brown eyes, thatch-like eyebrows, and a shiny bald dome surrounded by a fringe of lush gray hair. Young men, Misty noted, never smelled like Uncle Bernie. He smelled of cigars, bay rum, and something unidentifiable that might have been leather and might have been some essence sprayed on people like Uncle Bernie by expensive barbers. Misty's late Aunt Flo had

159

claimed that Uncle Bernie smelled purely of ill-gotten money.

When Uncle Bernie had come to Chicago while Misty was growing up, he used to take her off for the day with him. Their first stop was the Palmer House barbershop, where Uncle Bernie went to be shaved. Misty sat entranced while Uncle Bernie was wrapped in hot towels. She was enthralled when the barber approached with a mug of soap and a badger brush and painted Uncle Bernie's face with soap. After he was shaved, Uncle Bernie's fringe was carefully cut while a silent manicurist buffed his fingernails. When Uncle Bernie had been brushed off and had his jacket held out to him, he overtipped and then took Misty out to lunch at the Blackhawk Restaurant. Then he and Misty went to Soldier's Field, where Uncle Bernie watched the Catholic League football games and Misty hid herself in Uncle Bernie's coat to keep warm. In one rush, her childhood was brought back to her, and it felt odd to see her Uncle Bernie talking to the man who was now her husband.

"Great fellow you married, Misto," said Uncle Bernie. "Vincent here has been going on at great length about you. Brings a tear to this old eye to hear a fellow going on like that about his wife. I've been married a few times myself, Vincent. Have another cigar. In fact, have a box of 'em. I brought you kids some loot but it's still at the hotel. Married. Just think. It seems like yesterday that you and I were sitting in Soldier's Field, Misto."

"We used to go to the Palmer House first," said Misty.

"Ah, the Palmer House. Your father never approved. He used to get shaved in Hyde Park. He said: 'Bernie, can you tell me why you are exposing my little daughter, your niece, to the sight of money so badly spent?' I said to him: 'Fritz, the girl has to learn what real perfection looks like.' Well, kiddos, are you going to feed me, or am I going to feed you?"

"Uncle Bernie," said Misty, "are you coming out of hiding?"

"Oh, that," said Uncle Bernie. "Your pious family has that all blown out of proportion. I was never very crooked, Misto. Just a little crooked and it all had to do with taxes, anyway. A long time ago, my lawyers said to lie low, so I lay low in the Bahamas. Such a pleasant place I decided to stay, and it keeps me out of trouble. No, I'm here to see my platoon of lawyers and my squadron of accountants, and then I intend to go with your parents out to Medicine Stone and see the old place and the cousins. And, of course, I came to see you and this fellow you married. You turned out gorgeous, kid. Haven't seen you since your last year in college. That was at somebody's funeral. Whose funeral was it?"

"Aunt Flo," said Misty.

"Aunt Flo," said Uncle Bernie. "What a terrible pain she was. Let's say I take you out for supper. What'll it be? Small, *intime,* and expensive or small and full of gangsters?"

"Small and full of gangsters," said Vincent.

"That's the ticket, Vincent my boy," said Uncle Bernie.

Uncle Bernie took them to a hangout from his song-plugging days, a former speakeasy called the Firenze. The walls were decorated with shabby murals whose lurid colors had faded considerably. It was not, however, full of recognizable gangsters. It was filled with night watchmen, students, well-dressed couples, neighborhood locals, families feeding zuppa inglese to sleepy children, and young lovers drinking wine out of beer pitchers. During a lull, a prizefighter

161

with a large entourage walked in and was immediately seated.

At dinner, Vincent ate himself into a state of bliss. At home, he threw off his clothes and flopped into bed. He kissed Misty. He said: "Uncle Bernie is a top," and passed out.

Misty considered her sleeping husband. Living with Vincent, she thought, was often like living in a playhouse in which all the dolls and toys got along famously together. In the real world, Misty knew, people like Walter Cardworthy and Fritz Berkowitz waged social warfare. In the real world, when people like Misty and Vincent got married their parents were horrified and tried to stop the wedding. Or if that did not happen, the parents were icily polite but the newly wedded couple could not find a decent apartment, or one of them got sick, or the blood tests got scrambled. Living with Vincent made Misty realize that she had spent a good deal of her life ready to ward off some terrible low blow. She did not believe that most people were decent or kind. She had never believed that life went along smoothly. She did not believe that life left you alone to be happy in this world.

Vincent believed all these things. He thought that his happy vistas and Misty's grim vision fused into one full-balanced picture of the world.

The fact was that, while Misty was moral, Vincent was good. Watching him sleep it was revealed to Misty that the good do not necessarily have to maintain morality: they are born with it, while people like Misty, who were not good, had to strive mightily for goodness. That was what a moral system was: it helped you be good when you weren't very nice. From Vincent, Misty learned that goodness and stupidity were not necessarily linked. You could be good *and* smart.

Vincent did not judge: Vincent enjoyed. He enjoyed Uncle Bernie because Uncle Bernie was full of beans—because Uncle Bernie was there to be liked. Life was not as complicated as Misty had thought. With Vincent by her side, it was often as simple as Vincent thought.

Misty turned off the night-table lamp. With a little sigh, she turned over on her side, nestled against her husband, and went to sleep.

The next day, she sat at her desk musing on the subject of married life. Marriage, it turned out, was a series of small events. For example, this morning Vincent had put on his best tie and gone off to give a paper at the National Conservation and Technology Society. He was presenting the refined and streamlined plans for the small, compact machine that turned all household waste into mulch, sludge, or methane gas in quantities sufficient to power small machines, such as power mowers. This small system, he felt, could be expanded for use by a city: a multipurpose system that would turn refuse into a source of energy and municipal revenue.

When he came home tonight, he would be high and triumphant, as he always was when he delivered a paper.

Tonight was also to be the first meeting of Misty and Vincent's cousin Hester Gallinule, the soap-opera actress turned Broadway producer. Uncle Bernie was meeting with his lawyers and had promised to stop by after dinner with his wedding present.

"Why do we have to have all these relatives crawling around?" said Misty.

"Uncle Bernie isn't a relative," said Vincent. "Uncle Bernie is a divine emanation. And I promised that we would have cousin Hester for dinner."

"Will cousin Hester and Uncle Bernie get along?"

"Will they ever," said Vincent. "You just wait and see. Hester's crazy. She thinks if you have five small-time love affairs, it adds up to one big one. She's very gabby. You'll love her."

To Misty she sounded like a candidate for instant hatred, but she was Vincent's cousin. That was married life. Dishes were washed, laundry was done. You got up in the morning and went to work.

At work, you finished the Hispanic language project, delivered your research, and wrote an article that was scheduled to appear in *American Speech*. Then you were assigned to something called the Church in Life study, in which you measured the effects of foreign-language churches on the lives of their parishioners.

Married life had to do with getting used to being married. Vincent's advice was: "Just be married. That's how you get used to it. Where on earth did you get this sense of profound gloom from, anyway?"

"Life is never smooth to the great-granddaughter of tin peddlers who were kicked out of Russia," said Misty. "It's no accident that all my family is in one embattled profession or another. We're just waiting for the Cossacks to come back. When the Cossacks come to Connecticut, you'll understand."

Meanwhile, it was hard to feel much gloom at all, although to keep her balance. Misty clung to it wherever she found it. The Cossacks appeared at her office in the form of Denton McKay, whom she had never forgiven and watched with the wariness she felt she was the just inheritor of.

He sauntered into her office for a chat, propped himself on the corner of her desk, snooped at the grocery list she had on her blotter, and began to rearrange all her papers and paperclips.

"I hear you got married," said Denton. "Just got here and got married."

"Who says I got married?" said Misty.

"It's all over the office," said Denton. "One of the girls told me. There's an awful lot of girls here. Have you noticed? Lots and lots of them. What are they doing here, do you suppose?"

"You hired them to be paid saboteurs," said Misty.

"I did? No, I didn't. But that's not a bad idea. The co-opted saboteur. You hire 'em and they keep you alert. So. Who'd you marry?"

"Don't believe everything you hear," said Misty.

"Aw, come on. You married Vincent Cardworthy, right? I didn't even know you knew him. Are you that interested in garbage? You must be, if you married him. Brilliant fellow. Do you suppose there's a rule against married couples working here? I'll have to check. Anyway, I think it's wonderful. I like a tight ship. I guess we ought to give you something. What would you like?"

"A raise."

"No, no," said Denton. "Something for the two of you, like a martini pitcher."

"We have a martini pitcher. In fact, we have several."

"Well, then, something along the lines of a toaster," said Denton.

"We have three toasters," said Misty. "Why don't you think along the line of a priceless work of art?"

"Get serious," said Denton. "How about a silver candy dish? I have to get you something."

"I'll tell you what you can get," said Misty.

"What?"

"You can collect all those paperclips you've just arranged to form your initials and get out of here."

"Okay, okay," said Denton. "But I think a martini pitcher is just the thing."

That night, before his cousin Hester turned up, Vincent stood in the kitchen discussing his genius.

"I was brilliant," he said. "They loved me. I got three laughs, but most of the time they were sitting on the edge of their chairs."

"You are a disgusting ham," said Misty.

"That's only because I have true fervor. I am an apostle of thrift. A mulch machine in every home! Use your sewage to fuel your power mower! Heat your home with your own sludge!" He grabbed Misty. "One of these days, we're going to be very rich."

"Baste the duck," said Misty.

"Duck? What duck?"

"While you were off being a genius, I was buying a duck for dinner."

"And I have another idea," said Vincent. "After you finish the Church in Life study, we're going to collaborate on a garbage study. An ethnic study. We'll travel. We'll go to India and Africa. We will set out to discover how other cultures deal with refuse. We will analyze the implications of the language used to describe this problem." He bent down and poured orange juice over the duck. "What do you think?"

"I think you're still making your speech," said Misty.

"I am a genius," said Vincent. "Now please get out of here while I make one of my brilliant salads. And, as you will see, I am not only a genius. I am also thoughtful and kind. There is a cake box over there inside of which is the perfect dessert your astonishing husband has brought home."

Hester Gallinule was a tall, freckled forty-year-old woman with fuzzy hair and tinted glasses. She took off her coat as if revealing a monument. She wore a pink sweater, pink skirt, and boots so tight you could almost see her veins. She accepted a glass of white wine and collapsed against the sofa cushions.

"What a day," she said. "Sheer hell, except for tonight, of course. How divine to meet Vincent's wife." Hester had a wonderful, husky voice. "My voice," she explained, "has been feathered by my adenoids and tarred by my cigarettes." She smoked her cigarettes through a black holder.

"I don't have a present for you yet, darlings," she said. "I was out of the country when I got the announcement and I've been breaking my back to mount a new show. I simply can't get everything done."

Misty sat back on the couch enraptured. She had never had an older sister but Hester was like the older sister of every friend Misty had ever had. Those older sisters had gone to nightclubs. They wore pleated skirts, strapless evening dresses, and smelled of Shalimar. They carried in their handbags leather cases containing eyelash curlers, tubes of Persian Melon lipstick, and little pots of something that looked like Vaseline to rub on their eyebrows. They wore scanty underwear, Capri pants, and used ballet slippers as bedroom slippers. They had paid off Misty and her friends not to tell their mothers that they snuck cigarettes in the bathroom. Misty mentioned this to Hester.

"Darling, I am simply embedded in my generation," said Hester. "I feel so sorry for you young things. Think of what you've missed. Wrist corsages. Strapless bras. Garter belts. Every time I think about my adolescence I smell nail polish remover. We used to spend hours doing our nails. I still keep scrapbooks. I have all my old corsages and by now, of course, they're almost antiques. I even have one of my old strapless dresses. I've lugged it around all these years. You have to wear about ten petticoats with it. Of course, the petticoats disintegrated but the dress still stands. I used to wear it to masquerade balls. Jacques —that's my ex-husband—thought I was simply crazy but of course he was born all grown up. It's heaven to be a divorcée, depending of course on who you married. As Vincent will tell you, my ex-husband was a real son of a bitch."

"I liked him," said Vincent.

"You were a mere child at the time. A gawky teenager. Jacques probably looked like an adult to you. He was extremely dull and stupid and mulish. The worst type of French person," she said. "The sort that admires the English. French parsimony and English stuffiness. Too dreadful. When I was on 'Dangers of Midnight'—that was my soap opera, did Vincent tell you?—Jacques never watched it. He hated it. It shamed him in front of his stuffy friends. I, of course, loved it. It ran for years and years until I got bored and they killed me. I played Emma Jacklin, wife of Steve Jacklin, the young attorney. By the time I got killed, he was a middle-aged attorney. Anyway, he was cheating on me with a woman named Melba Patterson, who had an illegitimate son whose father was a complete mystery. Around the time I wanted to quit, they wrote in that the father was Steve Jacklin's father and the shock caused me to have a fatal car crash. Isn't that heavenly and retrogressive? By that time, Jacques was long gone and I went on tour with a play called *Very Fancy*. An appalling turkey. You've probably never heard of it. So, I figured enough was enough and that instead of acting I would take a little flyer and I invested in a musical about the occult called *Hocus Pocus,* which ran for seven years off-Broadway and made us all rich, rich,

rich. Now I'm a pillar of the theatrical community and Jacques can go to hell."

"What does Jacques do?" Misty asked.

"Money, darling," said Hester. "They say they're investment bankers and securities analysts, but they just make money. I remember when Jacques decided to buy a company. It made some part of a helicopter. I said: 'Jacques, you don't care about helicopters. You don't even like to fly.' He said: 'I don't care about the flying. I care about the money.' That's what he does. He makes money. A few years ago he married the dullest girl who ever lived but whose vast wealth compensated for how awful she was. Jacques of course wouldn't know the difference. God knows where he found her. Maybe he imported her. She made him a nice little bambino all his own and the nanny takes it to the park in an English pram. It's all very proper. I'm sure they have very traditional ideas about child rearing."

"It isn't called that anymore," said Vincent. "It's called parenting."

"In Jacques's case, it's called getting a nanny over from France," said Hester. "Let's eat."

During dinner, Hester discussed her lovers.

"Don't take this amiss," she said to Misty. "But I believe in having lovers. I used to have two. Now I've got three. One is a divine young thing. He just graduated from the film institute. It's so marvelous to be adored. He's so sweet and gloomy. He asks me to marry him about three times a week and when I say no because I'm almost old enough to be his mother, he thinks it's tragic. I find it poignant. The next I really can't discuss because he's too well known and very married and then there's Franz. You met Franz, Vincent. I've known him forever. He owns the Liebenthal Gallery and we go to Europe together. It all adds up.

I'm crazy about the little kid who adores me. I feel all sneaky and dangerous with my married friend, and Franz is my stability. Put it all together and you've got the ideal marriage."

Just as the coffee was served, Uncle Bernie appeared. He hugged Vincent, kissed Misty, and kissed Hester Gallinule's hand. Hester sat bolt upright in her chair.

Uncle Bernie was carrying an enormous box, which he set on the floor.

"It's your W.P.," he said. "Wedding present," he explained to Hester. "Open it up, kiddos."

Vincent and Misty bent to open the wrappings. Underneath the glossy white paper and ribbons was a dark blue box. Inside was what looked to be a fur coat.

"What is it?" said Vincent. He began to pull it out of its box. "It doesn't have any sleeves."

"What does it look like?" said Uncle Bernie.

"It looks like a bedspread made out of fur," said Vincent.

"You got it!" said Uncle Bernie. "That's exactly what it is. Fritz and Adalaide would never approve. I'll bet Misto doesn't either but if Uncle Bernie doesn't spoil you, who will?"

"This is the most wonderful thing I have ever seen in my life," said Vincent.

"And it's an energy saver," said Uncle Bernie. "That's right up your line of work, isn't it, Vincent my boy? Crawl underneath this thing and you'll never need a radiator again. Gorgeous, huh, kids?"

"I say let's go see how it looks," said Misty.

They trooped into the bedroom and agreed that the fur bedspread was a thing of beauty.

"Now for coffee," said Uncle Bernie. "So, you're in the theater, Hester. I used to be on the fringe of that myself. I was a song plugger. You're probably too young to know what that is."

"Sing Hester your song," said Vincent.

"I wrote a little ditty in the forties," said Uncle Bernie. "It was what they called a novelty number. I hoped it would start a fad, but it never amounted to more than a passing fancy. You really think Hester wants to hear a song called 'Dancing Chicken,' Vincent?"

"Hester does," said Hester.

Uncle Bernie stood up. Taking the lapels of his jacket in his hands, he sang "Dancing Chicken," did a little two-step, and flapped his jacket.

"That's the dance I made up to go with it," he said as he sat down.

Hester's back had ceased to touch her chair. She looked like a girl recently let out of convent school. The expression on her face did not reveal what the sight of Misty's bald, portly, beautifully dressed uncle flapping around the living room had done to her. Misty thought she was horrified. It turned out that she was not.

"Give me your jacket, Vincent," Hester said. "Okay, Uncle Bernie. Show me how it goes."

Hester and Uncle Bernie were about the same height, but Hester's boots gave her several more inches. Uncle Bernie twirled her around the living room. They flapped their jackets in unison and then tangoed into the kitchen.

"Oh, my God," said Misty. She was rubbing the bridge of her nose—a sure sign of distress.

"What's wrong?" said Vincent. "We have brought light and laughter into the hearts of our relatives."

Uncle Bernie and Hester tangoed back to the table, where they drank coffee and brandy and Hester took a puff of Uncle Bernie's cigar.

"It's time to go, kiddos," said Uncle Bernie. "I leave you to your vulgar bedspread. Now I'm going to escort your delectable cousin home."

"What a nightmare," said Misty, as she and Vincent cleared the table.

"Nightmare," said Vincent. "My God. It's a daydream come true. What a perfect match. Why didn't we think of it?"

"It seems a terrible idea," said Misty. "Uncle Bernie is a crook."

"Hester loves crooks. Besides, Uncle Bernie is only a little crooked. He said so himself. Hester loves a high roller. Honest to God, Misty. I sometimes think there's something wrong with you."

"There is."

"Well, what?"

"You believe in happy endings. I don't. You think everything is going to work out fine. I don't. You think everything is ducky. I don't."

"Why don't you?" said Vincent.

"Vincent," said Misty. "Sometimes I think you don't have the sense that God gave a chicken. Your family has been sleeping peacefully in Petrie since the beginning of time. I come from a family that fled the Czar's army, got their heads broken on picket lines, and has never slept peacefully anywhere."

"That may be true," said Vincent. "But you slept peacefully in Chicago. Your daddy grew up on a farm and as far as I can tell, your mother was brought up at the Art Institute. You never fled anyone's army. So explain yourself."

"It's cultural," said Misty.

"I'm for it," said Vincent. "We need each other. Neither of us is safe alone."

"Sometimes I think you don't understand how very different we are," said Misty.

"I realize every day," said Vincent. "But I think that love cures everything."

"You would," said Misty.

Nothing was heard of Uncle Bernie or Hester for several days. On the weekend, a formal thank-you note from Hester was received. In large, curly handwriting, she praised the duck, the charm of the apartment, her delight at Misty and Vincent's marriage and remarked that she and Uncle Bernie had been out dancing several times. A telephone call from Uncle Bernie confirmed this. He was just about to leave for Chicago and Medicine Stone and he called to say goodbye. He and Hester, he said, had found a number of wonderful places to dance: hotel roofs, Puerto Rican nightclubs, and shabby dance halls.

"We've been having a bang-up time," he said.

It was late Saturday morning and Vincent had gone off to a meeting of the Ecological Union. Misty was curled up on the couch watching the rain and reading the paper. She was about to take a nap when she was roused by the doorbell. She thought it might be Vincent coming back early, but it was not. It was Guido.

Misty and Guido had not had a private conversation since their first meetings at the Magna Charta office. Those two conversations had tacitly sealed the deal: unstated affection abounded between them—a nice, warm, and free-floating affirmation. One look at Guido told Misty that he was in trouble of some sort. This made her slightly nervous. Guido had probably come to see Vincent, but there was no Vincent to see.

"Vincent's out," she said. "Come in and have a cup of coffee."

"I know he's out," said Guido. "He's at the Ecological Union. I didn't come to see him. I came to see you."

Misty collected Guido's wet raincoat and umbrella and sat him down at the table for coffee.

"Oh," she said.

"Holly's pregnant," said Guido, wearily.

"Oh," said Misty. "Vincent doesn't know that."

"No," said Guido. "And I don't want him to know. I'm afraid I just can't face his smiles of delight at this wonderful news."

"I see."

"You probably do," said Guido. "I guess I thought I could count on you not to chirp with joy. I need to talk to someone, and that someone is you."

"It's Holly, isn't it?" said Misty.

Guido stood up and began to pace. He looked haggard.

"I want to have a baby," he said. "I want any old kind of baby. I want a kid I can teach to swim and take to the park and make up stories for. I want to take my kid to French restaurants on Saturdays and put wine in its water and put things to taste on its plate. I want to stay up all night when it gets sick and go to its piano recitals. I never knew how much I wanted to be a father before."

Misty asked, "What does Holly want?"

"I have no idea," said Guido. "She dropped this on me a few days ago. I didn't know she wanted a baby. I don't even know if she wants a baby now. She never said a thing about it. Now she's presented it to me as a fait accompli and she's involved in the details. For example, she wrote to a cabinetmaker in Maine about getting a crib made. I saw the letter. She's been making sketches of the back bedroom so we can turn it into a nursery."

"I'm afraid I don't see the problem," said Misty.

"I don't know how she feels," said Guido. "You don't know her. She's like a business person. She said: 'Guido, we're having a baby,' and that was that. I wanted to go out and tell everyone in the world, buy a box of cigars, fill the house with roses. You can't do that when you don't know whether your wife is glad or sad. She just makes plans. She hasn't said another word about it. She drops this meteor at my feet; it makes a big hole and she just sweeps it up, makes it level, and goes on."

He sat down and slumped in his chair, setting the coffee cup down a little too violently on its saucer. He pulled a cheroot out of his pocket and lit it. His hazel eyes looked liquid and troubled.

"Guido," said Misty. "Maybe you need to know too much."

"Vincent knows too much," said Guido. "It's not hard to tell how you feel. I'm living with a walled fortress."

"Vincent is living with a partially ruined walled fortress that is trying to get up the wherewithal for repairs," said Misty.

"I think she's going to leave me again," said Guido.

"What makes you think that?"

"I know her," said Guido. "It's time for her to retreat."

"Well, let her," said Misty. "From what I understand, she didn't leave you the first time. She just went away for a few weeks."

"That's leaving."

"Jesus, Guido. I thought I was marrying into an intelligent family. You are not married to *Woman*. You are married to one specific woman. That one specific woman behaves in one specific way. She needs to be by herself every once in a while. What difference does it make? Unless you don't trust her."

"It's not that I don't trust her. It's just that I don't understand and she can't explain."

"You don't understand because Holly isn't you," said Misty. "If *you* went off, it would be for some specific reason having to do with you and Holly. You can't believe that she can go off and not have *your* reasons. Well, she isn't you. She has reasons of her own. As long as she loves you and doesn't stay away for very long, why don't you leave her be? Having a baby is a big deal. Maybe she needs a little time to get used to it."

"This is a very disconcerting conversation," said Guido.

"You asked for it," said Misty.

"Don't tell Vincent for a bit, will you?" said Guido. "I'll tell him—but not until I get this thing straightened out."

"You and your friend Vincent are hopeless," said Misty. "There isn't anything to straighten out. Ask her if she's glad she's having a baby and then let her go."

"But what about me?" said Guido. "What about my right to fatherly joy? How about my feelings?"

"You'll get your big chance," said Misty. "Just wait till you have your baby in your arms and it drools all over your suit."

Holly *was* going off, and she was going off to get used to the idea of having a baby. Misty had been entirely right, and so had Guido in his choice of the word "retreat." Holly was going to a monastery. She had found an order of Anglican nuns and she was making a retreat.

"You don't have one ounce of religious feeling," said Guido.

"I may not have religious feelings, but I like a religious atmosphere," Holly said. "Besides, the thought of being pregnant makes me feel medieval. It's a contemplative order and I need silence. And

176

furthermore, I have an impulse to be around a lot of women."

"Really?" said Guido fiercely. "And how did you find out about these saintly women?"

"It's a famous place. I've always wanted to go. There's a retreat mistress, and there will be other women making retreats too."

Holly was lying on the sofa wrapped in a plaid rug. A tea tray was on the floor next to her with its flowered cup and saucer, pot, and jug of milk. A little glass plate held the remains of toast with honey and butter.

Holly made you think of painting, of composition, Guido thought. You could not look at her and not think of her elements: the flush on her cheek, her thick, silky hair, the contrast between her wrist and the cuff of her shirt. She looked warm, but not lazy. Holly knew how to clear the deck for action. She would find maternity clothes that looked just like her usual clothes. She would find perfect clothes for the baby. She would invent a diet for expectant mothers and fathers and when the baby came, she would invent a diet for it too. Guido had always found the sight of beautiful women with reading glasses or babies very moving. Soon he would come home to the sight of his beautiful wife and baby. If all had been equal, Guido would have been swooning with joy.

Next to the couch was a pile of books: a copy of *The Rule of St. Benedict, Diets for Mothers,* and a white-jacketed book entitled *Prenatal Serenity.* Holly worked fast, but she kept his joy in check. He wanted to fall on his knees and sing for gladness, but Holly was talking about her retreat.

"I can't think of a healthier place to be," she said. "They have lots of land, so the air is very clean. They grow all their own food. They have a farm, a vegetable garden, and a dairy. They make their own butter and cheese. They have a guest house for people like me. And it'll be good for the baby too. Dr. Margot Justis-Vorander in this book on prenatal serenity says that it is crucial for babies to spend the first weeks of their incipient life in real tranquillity. That's something very few people realize. The mother ought to be as serene as possible."

"What about the father?" said Guido.

"I have to work on impulse," said Holly. "Pregnancy seems to have its own instincts. I must have some real silence. It's good for the baby. Besides, you don't have to lug this baby around—I do. I have to get used to it and think about it. It's just a few weeks."

"How many is a few?" said Guido.

"The retreat is ten days but you can stay longer."

"You mean, *you* can stay longer," said Guido.

"Don't be ferocious, darling," said Holly. "After all, having a baby is serious business."

Serious business meant that Holly would not be back in ten days. It meant that she would come back when she felt like it. Guido was a brooder, not a sulker, but now he felt his options had been taken away from him. He sat down and sulked. Life was unfair to those who were just, he thought. No matter how maddening Holly was, he was forced by temperament to see her side—or what he thought her side might be if she had ever bothered to really explain herself. The fact was: she was having the baby and Guido was only a witness. Was his desire to keep her by his side the terrible possessiveness of an onlooker? Maybe he was jealous. Maybe all men were. Perhaps his present anger at Holly was really anger at his position: he had been present only at the conception. Now the mystery began and it was Holly's own.

Perhaps he did need to know too much. Perhaps he needed everything spelled out in big block letters. Holly was not an explainer. She was a contented accepter. How could life be so graceful and confusing at the same time?

"Don't look so stricken," said Holly. "Come curl up with me. A little love in the afternoon is probably very good for our incipient wonder child."

"I thought it had to have perfect serenity," said Guido.

"That simply means not being fraught," said Holly. "Not being caught up in the unnecessary tensions of modern life."

Guido stood up. He thought for a fleeting instant of how smug he had been to Vincent during Vincent's early courtship of Misty. Vincent had said, in desperation, "Sometimes I think it's love and sometimes I think it's sickness."

This seemed the heart of the matter to Guido. As Holly slid her arms around him, he was not sure which was which.

CHAPTER 8

HOLLY WENT OFF TO HER RETREAT EARLY one morning, carrying a plain black grip and wearing what she felt were appropriate clothes for an outsider at a monastery: black skirt, white shirt, gray sweater, and gray stockings. She had taken the diamonds out of her ears and wore tiny seed pearls. In her handbag she carried a copy of *The Rule of St. Benedict,* a bottle of vitamin pills, and Dr. Justis-Vorander's book on prenatal serenity. Watching her dress, Guido knew she would be the most chic of all possible retreatants.

As soon as she was gone, he hurried to his office where life no longer held any surprises. Betty Helen had come back, and Stanley had decided to stay on to help out. To Guido's amazement, Stanley and Betty Helen got on like a house afire. Stanley performed the services of errand boy, second typist, and proposal and manuscript reader. During the occasional afternoon lull, he liked to read the proposals to Guido, whose name he had shortened to "Guid."

"Okay," said Stanley. "Get this. This one says: 'Space and time are configurative modalities bound by their infinite essences. Shape alludes to happenstance within the context of essential boundlessness, hence the concept of accident. The artist works within invisible limitations which impinge on perception, energy, and their combination called work, which is not to be confused with "the work." ' Guess what this one is, Guid."

"That," said Guido, "is a proposal from a sculptor who wants to arrange a series of paving stones on a lawn."

"Close but no cigar," said Stanley. "It's from a potter who wants to duplicate 'accidental forms in nature.' "

"What does he say an accidental form in nature is?"

"Well, this guy says, for example: 'random events held together by formless ties making form out of unique structure.' "

"That means something like a puddle," said Guido.

"Yeah?" said Stanley. "This is really weird. It's a whole 'nother language."

"When I was your age," said Guido, "I used to read those things for my Uncle Giancarlo. That's why I'm so fluent. Of course, people weren't writing that way in large numbers so we got the usual family saga novel proposals, and poetic cycles about Cincinnati, and murals for schools. You know, sculptors who used chisels and poets who used words. When Uncle Giancarlo got a proposal like your accidental form in nature one, he used to take a red grease pencil and write across it: IF YOU CAN'T WRITE A COHERENT PROPOSAL, YOU CAN'T HAVE A GRANT. And then he'd send it back."

181

"And then what would happen?"

"Well, you'd either never hear from them again or they would have to rewrite it and face the fact that what they wanted to do was make a giant nail out of Styrofoam, and Uncle Giancarlo would write NO NO NO in red grease pencil and send it back. Then the fellow would get a grant from someone else. Uncle Giancarlo wanted to keep the Foundation on the conservative side. His motto was: no one ever said 'my five-year-old child can do better than that' about Raphael or Matisse."

"This is the basis for a new parlor game," said Stanley. "Like, I make one of these up and you have to guess what it is. Okay. What does this mean: socio-romantic stress entangled with the dailiness of human experience meld to produce an exit from repressive structures in an attempt to redefine parameters."

"That means: you're having trouble with your girlfriend and you want the afternoon off."

Stanley was awestruck. "That's amazing," he said.

"Just a job," said Guido.

"Not a job," said Stanley. "A force/completion modality expressed structurally in terms of repeated action."

"Get lost," said Guido.

Stanley's version of taking the afternoon off was to have a long lunch with Vincent, who was now established in his affections as a full cousin. Stanley was in need of guidance and no one had ever given it to him. His brother Muggs's only advice to him had been "Never mix drugs." And since Muggs lived in California as well as having been judged useless by Stanley, Vincent was an admirable older brother substitute.

"I've got this problem," he said to Vincent.

"You're too young to have problems," said Vincent.

"Well, I do. Just because I'm young is no reason not to take me seriously. I'm in what they call a lying situation. I mean, I lie to Sybel because she thinks I love her all the time, but, in fact, half the time I'm with her I think about Misty's friend Maria Teresa."

"Maria Teresa thinks you're a bug. She's too old for you," said Vincent.

"It's not *her,* man. Per se, I mean. It's the thought of her, see. I mean, Sybel is good for me. The food she eats has a lot of resistance. It makes you healthy. She makes me do these yoga exercises in the morning and then we meditate. I mean, she meditates, I just check out her feet and stuff, and don't pay any attention. Basically, I concentrate on Maria T. I make up love letters in Latin and stuff. I don't know. Sometimes I think it's because I'd like to eat ice cream once in a while without guilt, or maybe I don't really have the right feelings about Sybel. I mean, I feel I ought to be honest with her."

"It's never wise to be honest," said Vincent.

"Yeah? That's pretty sophisticated. I thought you were a real straight arrow. But, man, this is really getting to me. This morning Betty Helen said I had a gray aura, and usually it's yellow."

"Betty Helen?" said Vincent. "You discuss these things with Betty Helen?"

"No, man, I'm just saying what Betty Helen said about my aura."

"What does all this mean?" said Vincent sternly.

"Geez, Vince. Didn't you ever talk to her? She's really weird. She believes in spirituality. She sees auras and they tell you what kind of mental state you're in. Like for example she said Guido is usually light blue but he's turned a sort of dark, muddy purple color. And that makes sense what with Holly going into a convent."

Vincent stared at Stanley. "A what?"

183

"A convent," said Stanley. "Holly went into a convent."

"A what?"

"Don't keep saying that," said Stanley. "I heard Guido on the phone this morning with Holly's mother. Holly went into a convent."

"You sit here," said Vincent. "You just sit here and don't move. I'll be right back."

He walked angrily over to the bar and demanded to know where the public telephone was. He was directed to a wooden booth that was occupied by a nervous-looking young woman holding an address book and talking a mile a minute. Her face was to the wall so that Vincent's furious pacing did not catch her eye. After about two minutes, Vincent knocked on the glass.

"How long are you going to be?" he shouted.

"This is a very serious conversation," said the girl. "I'll be on for a little while."

"This is a public telephone!" shouted Vincent. "You are not supposed to make serious telephone calls."

"This is very important," snapped the girl.

"If you don't get out of there, I'll call the police," said Vincent. "This is a matter of life and death."

"Well, just a minute," said the girl. She murmured into the phone and then hung up.

"It's all yours," she said. "You may have ruined my life."

The booth smelled of French perfume. Vincent dialed Guido's number angrily.

"Stanley tells me that Holly has entered a convent," he said. "Just what is this all about?"

"I have no privacy," said Guido.

"Screw your privacy," said Vincent. "I'm your oldest friend."

"Holly went on a retreat," said Guido. "She found some tasteful monastery and off she went. She thinks

184

it's good for a baby to hang around in a serene atmosphere."

"What baby?" shouted Vincent.

"For God's sake, stop shouting," said Guido. "Holly is having a baby. Didn't Misty tell you?"

"How does Misty know?"

"I told her," said Guido. "Maybe I told her not to tell you. I can't remember. I was pretty upset."

"I think you'd better come over for dinner tonight," said Vincent. "I don't get this."

"It's the usual. Everything's wonderful. Holly's having a baby and she's gone off to commune with some Anglican nuns. I don't understand anything and I'm going to be a father."

"Congratulations," said Vincent. "That's actually wonderful. It's too bad I'm too furious to appreciate it. I'll see you tonight. Christ, I'd really like to break your neck."

"I'm going to be an uncle," said Vincent, sitting down. "Holly is having a baby."

"I thought she was going to be a nun," said Stanley. "Anyway, that doesn't make you an uncle. It makes you something like a third cousin once removed."

"It makes me an uncle because I will feel like an uncle," said Vincent. "And Holly has gone to a monastery on a retreat."

"Yeah?" said Stanley. "Far out. We used to have to read some of that monastic stuff when we studied Church Latin. Very weird. Jews don't have any of that hoo-ha. Geez, you look furious. Did you let Guido have it?"

"No," said Vincent. "I was angry, but I'm not now. Eat your lunch."

"Don't practice being an uncle on me, man," said Stanley. "I can see you're angry. I'd be angry if my best friend held out on me. Well, enough about you. What about me?"

"Your problems are mush," said Vincent. "Just wait till you grow up and have real problems. Meanwhile, my advice to you is to have some of that pastry for dessert. An éclair or two promotes clear thinking."

"Oh, yeah?" said Stanley. "In that case, I'll have an éclair and a Napoleon on the side."

Vincent left the office early and walked home alone. He wanted some time to himself to think things over. Guido had held out on him. Misty had held out on him. What was the reason for this? His companion on his walk was a deep sense of persecution. Had Guido and Misty discovered some insufficiency in him? Was he incapable of handling vital information? Was he so self-absorbed that no one told him anything anymore?

Or perhaps this was a trend. After all, Stanley felt he was holding out on Sybel. Who else, he wondered, was holding out on whom? He passed a row of brownstones whose lighted windows had always made him feel that lives of warmth and stability were conducted behind them. Now he wondered how many secrets were being kept by how many people in those houses. Which husbands were lying to their wives? Which wives were lying to their husbands?

At home Vincent sat down with a glass of whiskey. Best friends should tell each other important things, he thought. Having a baby was an important thing, especially when an uncle was involved. The whiskey warmed his chest and made him think that perhaps he was making a big deal out of nothing. He picked up a magazine from a basket next to the chair and began to look through it. Vincent was on the mailing list of every do-good institution in the country and he received all of their publications. The magazine he picked was produced by the Foundation for Human Fellowship. On its cover was a detail from a Bosch painting and the words: "Is the World Going to Hell?" Vincent was certain that it was: the warmth of the whiskey had worn off. *Human Fellowship*, as this magazine was called, had a monthly column containing a quote, and humanistic opinions about the quote. This month's was from Georg Simmel and read: "The farther individuals are removed from our most intimate personality, the more easily we can come to terms with their untruthfulness, both in a practical and in an intimate psychological sense—while if the few persons closest to us lie, life becomes unbearable."

Vincent threw the magazine on the floor. It was his wife who believed that there were no accidents. This quote was no accident. The few people closest to him had lied. Life was unbearable. He finished his whiskey in a fury.

When he heard the click of Misty's key in the lock, he leaped from his chair and stood in the hallway glowering. He did not say hello or kiss her. He watched her hang her coat up in the closet.

"Why are you standing in the hallway blocking my path and looking so petulant?" said Misty.

"I am tired of being lied to!" shouted Vincent. "I am tired of having my good nature taken advantage of. I am tired of being scorned as a cheery fool while the rest of you grownups go around being serious."

"So Guido spilled, huh?"

"So Guido spilled," said Vincent menacingly. "How coy. Yes, Guido spilled, because your cousin Stanley is an eavesdropper. Now I discover that my best friend and my wife have been sharing information to which I am not permitted access. Is that because I'm not deep enough to understand it? Is it because my temperament is too lighthearted to deal with these grim realities? If my best friend's wife is pregnant and I am about to be an uncle, am I not to be told?"

"Third cousin once removed," said Misty.

"And if my best friend's wife who is carrying my niece or nephew goes to a monastery, am I also not to be told?"

"A monastery?" said Misty. "Holly?"

"Ha!" said Vincent. "I see you don't know everything. Holly has gone on a retreat."

"How chic," said Misty.

"Is that chic?"

"It is now," said Misty. "I think you have real dramatic talent, Vincent. I think you ought to ask Hester if she can get you some acting work. I had no idea you were so Shakespearean."

"I am furious at you and Guido," said Vincent.

"So I see," said Misty. "Now if you will let me out of this hallway, I shall explain."

Vincent sat in his chair and waited. Misty did not speak. She simply looked at her husband quizzically.

"Spill," said Vincent.

"I will not speak from a stand," said Misty. "I will speak from your lap."

"No you don't," said Vincent. "You keep your feminine wiles off me."

"Nope," said Misty. She climbed into his lap and put her arms around him.

"You know what, Vincent?" she said. "You really are nicer than other people. You really do take the right things seriously. I'm just a small-timer. Guido came over on Saturday and I think he needed to talk to a woman. He was very upset because he isn't able to figure out how Holly feels about things and Holly doesn't talk. She just *does*. So she got pregnant, sprang it on him, and he went all to pieces. He asked me not to tell you because he felt so awful."

"And he assumed that I would come over all happiness and he wouldn't be able to stand it. Right?"

"Right. So here's the situation. Guido was waiting until he felt right enough to tell you, and you would have been happy in either case. That's love for you."

"Where do you fit into this neat equation?"

"Me?" said Misty. "I'm big time about small issues. Guido told me not to tell, and when someone tells you not to tell, that's sacred writ. Any thirteen-year-old girl knows that. It's teen honor and I have never outgrown it."

"Do you realize," said Vincent, "that this incident has broken down the barriers of trust? Do you know that when those closest to you lie, life becomes unbearable?"

"Of course I do," said Misty. "We read the same magazines. I'm like a dog with a bell when it comes to secrets. That shows you how undeveloped I am. If I had been big time, I would have told you, but you would have felt the same way, wouldn't you?"

"Certainly," said Vincent. "Mad at Guido and glad at the baby."

"Well, that's the problem with good people," said Misty. "You can't tell them anything."

"In that case," said Vincent, "there's no point in being good."

Guido appeared for dinner looking grim. Vincent was still furious and Misty was edgy. Politeness broke out on all sides. Dinner was finished off amidst a great deal of forced chatter, and when it was time for coffee Misty felt that she ought to retire to the drawing room for a cigar in order to leave the boys alone.

"Oh no you don't," said Vincent.

"Don't leave," said Guido.

"Are we going to sit around and discuss our clash of temperaments?" said Misty.

"Yes," said Vincent. "We are going to sit at this table and discuss that very thing. I will begin. You, Guido, have concealed vital information from me. You, Misty, have been an accomplice. Guido has failed to distinguish between his rotten mood and our friendship and you have failed to give up some teen-aged ideas you have about confidences."

He sat back in his chair and lit a cigar. Guido and Misty gave each other looks of pure relief. Once Vincent had aired his anger, he always forgot it. He was no longer angry and they both knew it.

It was now Guido's turn.

"If this makes you feel bad, think of how I feel. Holly gets pregnant without so much as a discussion. I didn't know she wanted a baby. She never said a word to me. From the way she behaves, you'd think the stork flew in the window and left the idea of a baby under one of her floral arrangements. Not a word! I can't believe she sprang this on me. It isn't that I don't want a baby. I do. But this is the twentieth century. We're a married couple. Aren't married couples supposed to discuss these things?"

"According to what rule?" said Misty.

"Would you spring a baby on me?" said Vincent.

"It's a pleasure to spring anything on you since you're such a goop," said Misty.

"She *sprang* it on me," said Guido.

"But you want a baby," said Vincent brightly. "And now you're going to have one. Why don't you just sit back and enjoy it?"

"It's not the baby," said Guido. "It's the idea of it. It's that Holly harbored this desire and didn't bother to tell me. We were supposed to talk about it together."

"How disgusting," said Misty. "Now it's my turn. You expect Holly to behave as you would behave. She doesn't and she never will. Did you ever for a second stop to think that maybe Holly already knew you wanted a baby and didn't want to have endless discussions about it? Maybe she wasn't up for one of those mechanical modern conversations about sperm. Maybe it was an accident and she thinks it's a happy accident. I can see your point and you're entitled to it. But you have to see Holly's and Holly is not you. Besides, Holly answers everything you think about the world and loves you too. You win both ways. You can brood with nothing very serious to brood about. You can think the universe is dark and full of awful surprises and you can be right and wrong at the same time. Holly is the perfect wife for you. If you were married to someone just like you, the two of you would sit around and discuss every tiny event in your past, present, and future and you'd never have any fun."

"If Holly is so perfect," said Guido, "why do I feel so awful?"

"Because what you wanted to happen happened, but not in the way you wanted it to," said Misty. "You didn't orchestrate it. In short, you are a spoiled brat."

"That isn't nice," said Vincent.

"It isn't," said Guido. "But it's true. Let's have something to drink."

They retired to the living room. Vincent brought out brandy and glasses. The three of them sat together on the couch, drinking. By the second round, they all felt rather mellow.

"Misty is allowed to say anything she wants," said Guido. "She's family."

"We are all family," said Vincent, for whom brandy and sentiment went hand in hand.

"I feel much better," said Guido, stretching his legs. "This is adult friendship."

"This is brandy," said Misty.

"What a materialist you are," said Guido. "I'm in

the company of my family and I'm feeling much happier than I have in weeks."

"It won't last," said Misty.

"What does it matter?" said Vincent. "We're all together. We're family and we're friends. I think that's the best thing in the world, and Guido does too."

"You boys," said Misty.

Holly came back in a little less than three weeks. Guido came home one evening to find her in the kitchen making dinner. She looked in radiant health.

"I thought I was supposed to come and pick you up," said Guido.

"I wanted to slip back unobtrusively," said Holly. She gave him a serene kiss and went on with dinner as if she had never left. She advised Guido that the meal was to be his favorite and that he must leave the kitchen at once.

"I'm not used to talking," she said. "I have to get used to it gradually."

Holly had left the place immaculate and Guido had kept it that way. There was almost no sign at all that she was back. Her clothes had all been folded or hung up and put away. But when Holly wasn't around, all the life went out of the place and Guido felt that he was living in the midst of a dead landscape. When Holly was gone, Guido kept all the lights on and still everything looked dim. With Holly back, the one nighttable lamp made the room look soft and warm.

At dinner Guido felt he was eating real food for the first time since she had left. Meals in restaurants, at other people's houses, or things he put together for himself did not taste real to Guido. Holly was a very pure cook, and nothing else tasted quite right to Guido.

Over coffee, Holly spoke about her experience with tranquillity.

"I haven't had a cup of coffee in three weeks," she said. "I completely forgot what a stimulant it is. And silence—it's amazing what not talking does. You keep silence at meals but someone reads to you. You don't talk during the day except for a little while in the afternoon. I heard a few spiritual lectures. But the amazing thing is the atmosphere. You just soak it in and realize how even if you're not a tense person as a rule, living in society makes you tense. I'm beginning to think that space absorbs silence or noise. For example, I got on an empty train to come home and it sat in the station for about fifteen minutes. There was no noise at all except the usual birds and dogs, but it didn't feel quiet. Whereas in the monastery, even when it's full of people it's completely hushed. I can't tell you how soothing it is. It made me wonder how to put more silence into normal life."

At this Guido's fork clattered loudly to his plate. The last three weeks had taken their toll. He was jumpy, nervous, and about to come down with a cold. His bones felt hot and his flesh felt cold. Blankets did not help. He did not want to put more silence into normal life. He did not want Holly to go off to a life of silence and leave him all alone. A little more quietude might kill him, he felt.

That night, he fell into a feverish sleep. He dreamed that Holly had gone away. This woke him up. He sat up in bed shivering. In the darkness he could see the ghostly shapes of the furniture. The bedroom looked like a seascape. He sank back into the pillows and drifted off. This time he dreamed that Holly had decided never to come back. He tossed unhappily until he felt her leg next to his. This made him feel better. He fell asleep and dreamed that Holly had entered a convent and that he would never see her again. The sense of loss and hopelessness in his dream was so acute it woke him up. He felt for Holly's leg, but Holly was not in bed.

She was sitting in a chair reading in the little pool of light cast by her reading lamp. Guido was half awake, still in the grip of his terrible dream. Holly looked very far off in the distance, canceled out by light. He tried to focus, but he could not.

It was four o'clock in the morning. He felt very feverish and spoke without meaning to.

"Holly," he said. "Please come back."

The light was flicked off. He heard her put the book back on her night table. Then her cool hand was on his forehead.

"Poor darling," she said. "You have a fever."

"Please come back," said Guido.

"I am back," said Holly.

"Just come back," said Guido. "Come back and don't leave me."

"I am back, darling," she said. "I haven't left. I'm right here. Now go to sleep."

PART THREE

CHAPTER 9

HOLLY HAD A COUSIN CALLED GEM—GEM
Jaspar. Gem was five years younger and Holly had
never paid much attention to her. When Holly was in
college, Gem was still playing field hockey and was
thus fixed in Holly's mind as a girl wearing a school
uniform.

Gem lived publicly in the world. When fashion
magazines did spreads about the proper clothes to
wear while sailing, Gem's photo was sure to turn up.
When lavish parties were reported by the newspapers,
Gem's name was always mentioned. In Holly's me-
ticulous address book, Gem took up a page and a
half. Holly hated crossing out addresses since it ruined
the precision of her script and Gem's peripatetic life
had caused her much small anguish on this account.
Holly believed that people ought to settle and she
wrote everyone down in ink. Gem had finally been
demoted to pencil.

Gem was one of those tall, crisp athletic girls who

look slightly cross-eyed from a distance but not up close. She had been sent to school in France and had made a pass at going to college but had only floated through the many institutions of higher learning to which she had been sent. Somewhere along the line she had been married to a man named Clifford van Allen. They had been married in Switzerland and had set about traveling. Clifford raced horses and cars. These were his only interests. Somewhere along the line he and Gem had gotten divorced and Gem had set about on a course of self-improvement. She went to fashion school, took classes in architectural drawing, and put in four months at interpreters school finding out if her French was good enough for simultaneous translation at the United Nations. It was not. These occupations took up the spring and fall. Otherwise, Gem summered and wintered. She sailed in the summer and skied in the winter, mostly abroad.

When Gem came to visit, her muddy riding boots stood outside the door of wherever she stayed and in fine weather her jodhpurs were hung over the railings. Gem traveled heavy. She carried boots, an iron bootjack, and frequently brought along her saddle, as well as a collapsible stainless-steel saddle rack. There was no occasion for which Gem did not have proper clothing and equipment. Life made certain demands on Gem: she needed space for her downhill skis as well as her cross-country skis, for her ski boots and skates, for her hiking boots, rock-climbing gear, sailing shoes, and hunting tack.

Holly and Guido had not seen her since their marriage, but her whereabouts had been documented by a series of postcards and scribbled messages that bore a resemblance to letters but were more like outpourings. Holly did not know why she was the recipient of Gem's innermost thoughts. She marked it down to the fact that she was Gem's only female cousin. Guido marked it down to the fact that Gem probably had no one else to send these messages to.

One evening Guido came home and tripped over a pair of riding boots. In the living room, he found Gem drinking a cup of tea and staring into the handmade crib that contained the six-month-old Juliana Sturgis Morris.

These days when Guido put his key into the lock, he knew what to expect: the scene he had hoped to witness—his beautiful wife and baby communing on the sofa. Having a baby made life more sure.

Besides, Holly's pregnancy had changed things. If she behaved mysteriously, there was a reason for it. If she burst into tears or stopped speaking, there was a cause. The baby, in fact, drew them together. Guido had assumed that Holly would hate being pregnant, but she did not. When she felt the baby kick, she called Guido to her side so he could feel it too. If Guido had ever wanted her to talk, she fulfilled his wildest dreams. She felt she was in the midst of a miraculous process that she described in minute detail. She talked about the mystery of life. She lectured Guido on dietary purity and would not allow him to smoke his cigars in the same room with her.

"You can't smoke in Juliana's presence until she is three," said Holly after the delivery.

For the first few days of Juliana's life, Guido was reluctant to go to work. He hung around the hospital with his nose pressed against the glass window of the nursery, staring at his daughter. The rest of the time he spent in Holly's room holding her hand, watching her sleep, or reading out loud to her from one of the pile of books on infancy she kept on her hospital night table.

One afternoon, she burst into tears. "I'm terrified to take her home," said Holly. "I'll make awful mistakes.

She'll get sick. She'll turn into a resentful teenager. Then she'll run away to a potato farm commune in the Southwest and it will all be my fault."

At this point, it was decided that a baby nurse was a very high priority. The next morning, Guido was confronted by a tall, middle-aged woman with short gray hair. She was sitting next to Holly's bed conversing earnestly. Her name was Ruth Binnenstock and she was an infant psychologist as well as a pediatric nurse.

"But babies just eat and sleep. Aren't they too young to have a psychology?" said Guido.

"I must explain," said Ruth Binnenstock. "I deal with sick babies, odd babies, hyperkinetic babies, babies who are about to undergo surgery. Since my own children are teenagers, I rent myself out once a year to spend some time with a normal baby. If I don't do that, I feel I lose the touch. Now, let's see yours."

Juliana was brought forth from the nursery wearing for the occasion a smock with tulips painted on it. Ruth Binnenstock held her up. Juliana looked at her with a clear, level gaze and then stuck out her tongue. Ruth Binnenstock stuck her tongue out at Juliana. Juliana squeezed her eyes closed and then began to coo. Ruth Binnenstock cooed back. Juliana smiled.

"It says in one of those books that when they smile in infancy it's only gas," said Guido.

"What idiocy," said Ruth Binnenstock. "People don't have the proper respect for babies. Babies are geniuses. They know everything. They want to know everything. This one is just perfect. Let me tell you something. Science doesn't know beans about babies."

Holly had indeed produced a stylish baby. This child had been delivered by Caesarean section and when put on display had been the most beautiful baby in the nursery.

Vincent and Misty had gone to view it. Babies

were all "it" to Misty until they wore clothes that more clearly identified them. She was not much of a fan of babies although she understood that when one of them happened to be yours, you found their little wrinkles and red faces perfectly enthralling. She and Vincent had stood at the big glass window on the maternity floor and surveyed a number of wrinkled babies.

"See that one?" said a man next to Vincent. He pointed to an enormous infant who was not only red, but also black and blue.

"That's mine," said the man. "Will you look at that brute? High forceps. Makes 'em look like they just went fifteen rounds."

One of these babies was not red and did not howl but lay in its crib looking intelligently around it with a sweet smile on its little face. This baby had a mop of curly black hair and looked exactly like a sugar baby.

"That's the one," said Misty.

"How can you tell?" said Vincent.

"The others are wrinkled," said Misty. "Holly's is pressed. Besides, you can always tell a Caesarean because they don't get all mangled up in the birth canal. Holly told me on the phone this morning that she had wanted natural childbirth but she was glad it was Caesarean because there's no birth trauma and the baby's introduction to life is more serene."

Finally, it was time to bring Juliana home. The crib had been delivered by the cabinetmaker in Maine. The back bedroom had been turned into a pale peach nursery. In the name of serenity, all grandparents had been temporarily banned, but they had sent their blessings in the form of mobiles to hang over the crib, night-lights, a metal cat under a glass bell that glowed in the dark, and a small Degas drawing.

Guido was sent reluctantly to work while Holly stayed at home to be schooled in the arts of mothering by Ruth Binnenstock.

"I am a failure," said Holly one afternoon. She and Ruth were drinking tea while Juliana took a nap. "I thought when you had a baby, you knew what to do."

"Nonsense," said Ruth Binnenstock. "Maternal wisdom is delivered with the passing of years, not with the baby. I say, simply follow your impulses. Try to think of what you would like if *you* were a baby. And never forget that you were one. Now, why did you decide to go on a retreat?"

"I wanted to be quiet. I wanted to be somewhere plain and simple with a lot of women around and I couldn't figure out where in the world I would find any kind of silence like that except at a monastery."

"Exactly my point," said Ruth Binnenstock. "You followed your impulses and they were right. If there were more retreats and more expectant mothers who went on them, I could work up quite an elegant study. I think you'll do just fine. Your impulse led you to Margot Justis-Vorander. I like to see a mother reading *Prenatal Serenity*. A fine book. A fine woman. I studied with her. Very brilliant and very humane. What this all boils down to is: when it comes to babies, never be afraid to make a fool of yourself. Mr. Morris will have no trouble on that score. I have never seen such a doting father—and I've seen enough fathers to last me several lifetimes. Coo when she coos. Crawl when she crawls. That's all a parent needs to know. They're only like this for a little while. Your worries will come much later on. But for now, take advantage. Get down on the floor and play with her. You happen to be very lucky. Juliana is a wonderful, kind baby. I've had babies puke and kick and spit out of pure spite. They have characters even at this

201

age. This one I want to stay in touch with. Once a year I will expect a dinner invitation. Besides, this baby is going to get the world's best food. I see you have been practicing making zwieback. I took a piece for breakfast this morning. Quite delicious."

When Juliana was put on a blanket on the floor to wriggle her arms and legs, Ruth Binnenstock wriggled along with her. When she cooed, Ruth cooed too. When Juliana sang, Ruth sang along. The sound of Juliana singing drove Guido into a frenzy of love. She sang in a high, piping voice that Ruth Binnenstock could almost imitate.

After a month and a half, Ruth Binnenstock decided that Holly and Guido knew all they needed to know and she began to pack.

"You can't leave," said Holly. "I'm too terrified."

"Nonsense," said Ruth. "If you get scared, just call me. But believe me, this baby of yours is a dream. She's perfectly fine. If there's any problem, it'll be yours, not hers."

Juliana didn't seem to mind when Ruth left, but Guido and Holly were crushed.

"It isn't that Ruth understands babies," said Holly. "She *is* babies."

"Alone at last," said Guido. "Don't look so stricken. Where's my kid?"

"She was taking a nap, but I think I just heard her."

"I'll go get her," said Guido.

"Be careful," said Holly.

"Get a grip on yourself, woman," said Guido. "Ruth said not to worry. Ruth says to coo when she coos, so I'll bring her in here and we'll coo together."

Juliana slept in a football jersey given to her by Vincent and Misty, which made her look almost unbearably adorable.

"Look at this beauty," said Guido. He held Juliana in his arms. He was terrified. "Now what do I do?"

"You put her on the couch next to me," said Holly, "and then you sit down next to her. Then we coo and appreciate her."

Holly and Guido were in great awe of their offspring. One or the other of them was constantly hanging over her crib, staring at her.

"We are treating this child like the Infant of Prague," said Guido.

"Ruth says that awe is an appropriate response," said Holly. "Besides, we have a sweet-tempered baby. Ruth says some babies cry all day and all night long. Our baby cries only when it's necessary. Some mothers are exhausted all the time. I'm exhausted only part of the time. Look at what gorgeous feet she has."

"She has beautiful little Renaissance feet," said Guido. Neither had taken an eye off Juliana, who lay almost perfectly still, taking adulation in stride.

As soon as Juliana had established a schedule for herself and Holly and Guido were a little less exhausted, Holly decided to have a dinner party in order to bring Juliana closer to the lives of Vincent and Misty. They had been permitted short visits, but now it was time to make an evening of it.

Before dinner, they all congregated in the living room. Juliana was placed on a quilt, where she wriggled happily. Holly and Guido demonstrated Ruth Binnenstock's precepts and when Vincent gave it a try, he found he was not half bad at wriggling. Misty was not much of a wriggler, so she waltzed Juliana around the room. Juliana found this very entertaining. Then they all sang to her. Guido sang her a song of his childhood. Holly sang Cole Porter. Vincent held her on his knee and sang "Lazybones." Misty took over and sang "Dancing Chicken" and flapped Juliana's arms.

"All adult conversation has been suspended," said Holly.

"This is the only baby I have ever seen who can be judged by adult standards of beauty," said Guido.

"Fatherhood takes away all modesty and propriety," said Holly. "Now you and Vincent can smoke your cigars. Juliana needs a few minutes of quiet after all this excitement and then I'm going to feed you."

At dinner, the conversation centered largely around Juliana.

"Betty Helen sent a present," said Guido to Vincent. "She knitted a little yellow coat and told me that babies were love incarnate."

"How would she know?" said Vincent. "Having never been one herself."

"Now, Vincent," said Holly. "Betty Helen is extremely kind. She called me up and told me that if I wanted she would come over and read Juliana's aura. She said Guido's aura was golden the day he came back to work after Juliana was born."

"I told you she was weird," said Vincent.

"Stanley says that when the time comes, he'll be very happy to give Juliana Latin lessons," said Misty.

"Having babies is wonderful," said Holly dreamily. "It's really quite stupefying. I feel I should be given the Nobel Prize. I can't wait until you two have one."

"If we ever have a baby," said Misty, "it will have my temperament and no one will want to come and see it. When it grows up, it will have Uncle Bernie's criminal tendencies and will cause great scandal."

"I think it's a wonderful idea," said Vincent. "Besides, you promised me that someday we would have a little Communist of our very own."

By the time Gem turned up, Juliana had turned from a beautiful infant into a ravishing one. Gem was not interested in babies. She claimed to know nothing about them and to prove it she unwrapped her present, which was a little china pig—just the right size for a baby to swallow.

When Guido entered the living room, both Holly and Juliana were half asleep. Gem had been talking all afternoon and Holly was now afog with names and places. Was it in Chile that Gem had gone skiing and discovered the lost places in her own consciousness? Or was it in Gstaad that she had met the Utopian psychologist who had told her about the lost places in her own consciousness? Did she have the affair with the journalist in France? Or was he a French journalist she had met in South America?

Gem had her own time scheme. If she said she was staying for two weeks, it meant that people would telephone her at your number for two weeks but Gem would hardly be there. In New York, for example, the country houses of a great many people Gem referred to only by last names were open to her. She was careful to leave the telephone number of these country friends on a pad in case any of her city friends wished to contact her. They did, in large numbers.

After her arrival, she was gone for three days, back for one, off for the weekend, and back for the evening. On that evening, Holly invited Misty and Vincent for dinner.

Juliana had been put to bed, and the five sat around the dinner table. Misty wore on her face an expression that Vincent called "the only Jew at the dinner table look." She was almost entirely silent. Vincent assumed that Misty did not approve of Gem, and that that was the occasion for the look. But it was not. For the first time in her life, Misty was mesmerized with jealousy.

205

Gem was every dog breeder Vincent had ever fallen in love with.

"I've just got to locate myself," Gem was saying. "All this traveling. All that luggage. When I was in Portugal, after I got back from Brittany, I realized that half my luggage was scattered over Europe and when I met Pablo Ruba—he's the psychoanalyst—I realized that life really is like a painting. I mean, if it's scattered here and there, it doesn't hold up as a coherent statement. So I've just got to locate myself and I think I ought to have a base. New York is it, I think. Did I tell you about this little house I saw? It's a carriage house and I think I'm going to rent it. It needs a lot of repairs but there's an option to buy. And it's a perfect place to work."

"Work?" said Guido.

"I didn't tell you about my wonderful plan," said Gem. "Well, when I was in London last month, I met this poet and he started me keeping a journal. I'd love to show it to you, Holly. I think you'd really understand it. Anyway, he sent me to a friend of his. You know him, Guido. Charles Redevere."

Guido nodded. Only Juliana did not know who Charles Redevere was.

"Well, he runs this seminar at the New York Poetry Society," said Gem. "And I'm going to be one of his students. I mean, I don't think that the poetic nature is everyone's inheritance, but I think the thing is that you've got to see if it's yours or not. When I was at Grandma's in Moss Hill, I used to ride over to that little chapel and just sit in there with my notebook. I thought maybe I would buy it and restore it. But then I thought, the country is for the luxury of calming down from something. The something is the city. So here I am. Now what do you do, Vincent?"

If he says "I'm in garbage," it's all over, thought Misty.

"Misty and I work at the Board of City Planning," Vincent said. "I'm a statistician, basically. I do studies of urban sanitation problems. Misty does language studies."

"How intriguing," said Gem. "Last year when I was in Greece I saw people dumping all sorts of stuff into the Mediterranean. And that doesn't have any tide, does it? Can you imagine all those island people dumping all that stuff into a body of water without tides? You ought to go see it, Vincent. Now, I've got to make a few telephone calls before it's too late, but I'm going to ask all of you if you'd like to go fishing this weekend. I have a friend with a boat and he's dying to go fishing for stripers. What about it?"

"We're having the invasion of the mothers-in-law," said Guido. "They're coming to slobber over our daughter."

"Why, that's perfect," said Gem. "Juliana can stay here and you can get away for the weekend."

"Fishing," said Vincent. "I haven't been fishing for years. Let's go. Misty says she's only fished for smelts."

"A weekend away would be nice," said Guido.

At this, Misty began to yawn. Gem went off to make her telephone calls. It was arranged that they would go fishing. With that, they cleared the table, and Vincent took Misty home.

"I don't want to go fishing," said Misty the next evening. "I have nothing to wear. You go."

"I'm glad you said you have nothing to wear," said Vincent. "I have bought you a pair of gum boots. Look, they're yellow. I saw them today and I thought they had your name on them."

"You thought my name was on a pair of yellow gum boots?"

"I did. Now put them on," said Vincent.

"I don't want to put them on. I don't want to wear gum boots. I don't want to go fishing. I want to be left alone."

"Just put them on for a second," said Vincent. "Get used to them. Fishing is a wonderful thing to do. You'll love it."

"I hate it," said Misty. "I hated it when my father took me fishing for smelts. All those creepy business-men with their fishing rods and their business suits standing on the rocks across from Buckingham Fountain with their disgusting fishing gear catching those revolting little fish."

"Did you catch any?"

"Daddy caught one. He put it in a jar and brought it home and let it swim in the sink. Then he fried it."

"How was it?"

"It was disgusting, like these boots. I won't go."

"You don't have to go fishing," said Vincent. "But you have to come for the weekend. You've never been to Salt Harbor and that's where we're going. We're staying at Scott's Fisherman's Inn. The reserva-tions are made. You can walk on the beach and mut-ter to yourself."

The week seemed very long to Misty. She was glad that Vincent's schedule was crowded so that he could not see what a horrible state she was in. At night she had terrible dreams in which she seemed to have shrunk to the size of a catsup bottle and was huddled in corners watching Gem, who was as large as an equestrian statue. She had dreams in which Vincent passed her on the street without noticing her. She had dreams in which Vincent was married to Gem.

It was one thing to theorize, Misty knew, but quite

another to live. Misty's theories looked down on the second-rate emotions such as jealousy. Since she had never felt it before, she had dismissed it as unworthy of feeling. Now she was in the grip of it. She stared it straight in the face and saw that the condition that jealousy covered was simply envy mixed with fear.

Gem stood for something—something effortless. Something that did not have to invent a personality in order to get by. Gem lived with an air of casual assurance. The world, Gem knew, would work for her. A million silkworms would lay down their lives so that Gem might have a shirt. Grooms went home to small, mortgaged homes so that Gem might stable her horse, and horses would be broken so that Gem might ride. Innumerable workers slaved anonymously so that Gem might be properly equipped. All Gem had to do was be, and doors opened to her.

Misty felt that life was a battle. You had to fight and think. You had to hack your way through life with your intelligence as a machete cutting down what obstacles you could. You were born knowing nothing: you had to fight for what you knew.

Even Vincent, whose effortless optimism was partly the product of hard work, fought. He fought at the Board. He fought government agencies and town councils. He sweated over his articles. Even Holly worked: she worked to make life sweet. Any reservations Misty might have lined up against Holly had been dispelled at her wedding breakfast. The sight of all that work and care made her realize what Holly's fight was: she fought to keep the ugly, chaotic world at bay and to keep a sweet, pretty corner to live in.

But Gem neither toiled nor spun. Gem made Misty feel that achievement was cheap in the face of that effortlessness. And Gem threw her. She had appeared at the wrong time. Misty was beginning to learn how much Vincent meant to her. She no longer thought of herself alone. She thought of herself and Vincent. She shopped as naturally for two as she had shopped for one. Every once in a while, she woke out of a deep sleep to realize how awful life would be without him. Gem stood for a part of Vincent that was not second nature to Misty—the part that was sporty and larky and on cheerful terms with the world, the part that had grown up sailing and fishing. Suppose Vincent got tired of someone who was not second nature to him?

Misty slunk around the office, breaking pencils, throwing her coat on the floor, and swearing over her calculator. She hated not working well. She hated having her mind cluttered. She was constantly afraid that she might burst into tears.

"Just looking at you makes my teeth chatter," said Maria Teresa Warner on Friday morning. "What's your story?"

"I'm going fishing," said Misty.

"Why has that made you so impossible?" said Maria Teresa. "I wish I were going fishing."

"Then you go," snarled Misty.

"Now, now," said Maria Teresa. "Is that any way to treat a little ray of sunshine like myself?"

"Why don't you get out of here?" said Misty. "Or sit down."

"I hate a gloomy person who lashes out," said Maria Teresa. "Who are you going fishing with?"

"Vincent, Guido, Holly, and Holly's cousin Gem."

"Ah," said Maria Teresa. "Gem. I've never heard that name before. Is it Gem who's putting you into such a foul mood? I see it is. What's *her* story?"

"Gem is every girl Vincent ever fell in love with rolled into one," said Misty.

"And so you see them all as a nice tidy picture with no place for you, right?" said Maria Teresa.

"How do you know that?" said Misty.

"Vincent told me once that you have an expression called 'the only Jew at the dinner table,' " said Maria Teresa. "You ought to try being Irish Catholic if you want to feel left out. I went to a dinner party the other night and everyone started fighting with me about transsubstantiation."

"It's not the same."

"Oh, it is too. And it doesn't make any difference. Everyone is not supposed to fit. St. Teresa says that God saw to it that she was always treated kindly everywhere although the only service she ever rendered him was to be what she was."

"So what?"

"So, God loves you more than you love yourself," said Maria Teresa. "A nun told me that in high school, and she was right."

"And God loves the poor because he made so many of them," said Misty. "So what?"

"So, you are not counting your blessings. You are having scruples, which is a very bad thing. Vincent loves you. You love him. Holly has a cousin and you're all going fishing."

"You don't understand," said Misty.

"I don't," said Maria Teresa. "Are you honestly jealous?"

"Yes."

"Well, gee whiz. You jealous. It's probably good for you. Did you ever discuss this with Holly? She knows her cousin and she knows Vincent."

"Friendship is not possible between two women one of whom is very well dressed," said Misty.

"Very true," said Maria Teresa. "Now let's change the subject. I am now getting a letter a week in Latin from your cousin Stanley. Would you please tell him that the only Latin I remember is the Paternoster?"

"You tell him," said Misty. "I'm very glad he writes

211

to you. It keeps him away from that horrible little Sybel."

"Thanks a lot," said Maria Teresa. "I'm getting out of here. You can be gloomy by yourself. Remember what St. Teresa said: 'Never compare one person to another.' Comparisons are odious. That goes for you and Gem. But just think. If this Gem is hateful and you're going fishing, you can always drown her."

They drove out to Salt Harbor early Friday evening. Gem and her companion were to meet them at Scott's Fisherman's Inn for dinner. In the car, they tried to figure out the name of Gem's companion. Holly remembered it as Raymond. Guido remembered it as Deering although he thought he also remembered Gem calling him Perkins.

With the exception of Misty, they were all in high spirits. Vincent had had a difficult week and was glad it was over. Guido had solved two pressing Foundation problems and Holly said that she felt strangely lightheaded.

"This is the first time I've been away from Juliana since she was born," she said. "Suddenly, I feel very young and strange. I'm going to end up calling home every five minutes."

"The mothers-in-law have landed, I assume," said Vincent.

"In force. With large numbers of packages. Trillions of toys," said Guido. "Juliana will be a spoiled brat when we get back. You should have seen her. Holly thought she would cry when we left but the only one who cried was Holly. Juliana looked like a little girl Buddha, only thinner. Our two mothers were practically prostrate before her."

The car sped across the dark highway. Misty fell

asleep against Vincent's shoulder. When she woke up, she saw stars against the black sky.

"We'll be there in half an hour," said Vincent. "Roll down the window, Guido. I want some salt air."

At dinner, the name of Gem's companion was not revealed. Gem called him Raymond, Deering, and Perkins alternately and he responded to all. He was a large man with a bulky frame, spindly legs, and lank, almost greenish-yellow hair.

They sat eating clam chowder and fried flounder in the dining room of Scott's Fisherman's Inn while Gem and her companion conversed.

"I moved into that house," she said. "That little carriage house. It's perfect, isn't it, Raymond?"

"Right-o."

"And I'm having Bucky shipped up to the Central Park Stables, aren't I, Deering?"

"Absolutely."

"Who's Bucky?" said Vincent.

"My horse," said Gem. "My new one. My old one died. My little hunter, Gretchen. She was my horse when I was a teenager. She was my oldest friend. I took her out for a ride to celebrate getting my divorce, and when I went to bed her down that night, she was dead. Dead marriage, dead horse, I said to myself. I cried and cried and when Lou Petroldi's Dead Stock Service came and took her away and I saw them hoist her onto the truck, I said: 'That's the end of my childhood.'"

"You ought to write that, Gem," said Gem's companion.

"I put it in my journal," Gem said.

At the end of dinner, plans were made. The next morning at ten o'clock they were to meet at the dock and board the boat that would take them fishing in the tidal rip.

"Right-o," said Gem's friend. "Four bells, got it? I've got to rattle the bushes for some extra lures." He took Gem's arm and escorted her out into the night.

Vincent flopped down on the double bed and sighed.

"Horizontal at last," he said. "What does 'rattle the bushes' mean, I wonder? What does 'ginormous' mean? He said the striped bass were ginormous."

"It obviously means big," said Misty.

"I feel like a fish," said Vincent. "I feel like a big, ginormous fish too exhausted to move a flipper. I am now going to rattle this pillow and go to sleep." He threw off his clothes and got into bed, rolling the blankets up under his chin.

"It's cold in here," he said. "Would you please hop in here immediately? A person could freeze waiting for his wife to keep him warm."

The next morning, Misty was up when the light woke her. It was seven o'clock. The sky was a bright gray and the water was dark blue. Under the covers, Vincent smiled as he slept. He claimed to have a recurrent dream about a computer—a very complicated dream full of jokes. He found sleep very entertaining for this reason. Misty had often heard him chuckling in the morning, but when he got up, he could never remember any of the particulars.

Misty wrapped herself in her coat and walked down to the water. The beach curved, like a cup. The tide was low. She walked with her hands in her pockets, thinking about Vincent.

The big surprise that marriage to Vincent had sprung on her was contentment. She had moments of desolation and moments of great joy, but underneath was some steady current of feeling. Misty's propensity toward pessimism and Vincent's toward optimism really did complement. Vincent was no less cheerful, and Misty was only slightly less judgmental, but they seemed to have formed a third person who smoothed out their edges and made life together possible and profitable. Misty excepted Vincent from the rest of humankind. He had his faults, but he was genuinely kind and true. He played fair and was generous. The difference between them was that Vincent really did believe that things worked out for the best and Misty did not. In Misty's world, the happy, comfortable, intelligent wife is left by a good, well-intentioned dummy who goes off with a woman whose childhood was ended by a dead horse.

On the far side of the beach, a speck of red appeared. It drew closer. It was Gem's companion dressed in bright red foul weather gear.

"What ho!" he shouted.

Misty was not certain how this greeting was properly answered. She said good morning. They began to walk together.

"What's your name, anyway?" she said.

"John," said the man.

"Gem doesn't call you that," said Misty.

"Gem likes to call a person by all his names. My name is John Raymond Deering Perkins."

"That certainly explains it," said Misty.

"Gem doesn't introduce," said John Perkins. "Ripping day, what?"

"What?"

"Bloody gorgeous out, no?"

"Yes," said Misty.

"Say what?" said John Perkins. "Are you married to that one or the other one?"

"The other one," said Misty.

"Difficult to know. Gem doesn't introduce."

"Have you known Gem a long time?"

"No, I haven't actually. Knew her husband, Clifford van Allen. Ingenious fellow that. Raced cars and horses. Does international finance now, whatever that means anymore."

Misty detected a slight drawl in his voice.

"Where are you from?" she asked.

"Eastern Shore," he said. "Maryland, what. Have you had breakfast? Let's go to the inn for a jolt of java."

He took her arm and led her up the steps to the inn. Misty cursed the day that she had stopped carrying a pencil and paper. She wanted to keep him talking but was not sure how to do it. It turned out he didn't need much prompting.

"Ghastly road that Harbor highway," he said. "Wizard prangs all over the place. Ices in winter, fogs in summer. Still, fabulous fishing out in the rip. Ginormous stripers. Come sit down."

They sat at a little table and Misty ordered coffee.

"What, no breakfast?" he said. "Why, you've got to grease the gullet."

"I don't eat breakfast."

"Most sensible thing, probably. Nasty habit, breakfast. Can't function on an empty stomach."

While he waited for his eggs, he began to discuss Gem's ex-husband, Clifford van Allen.

"After the bust-up, poor Cliff just lay doggo," he said. Misty kept perfectly still. As he spoke, her lips almost moved, memorizing. Even the most metaphysical linguist perks up as a new language is invented.

"Just lay doggo," he continued. "Terrible thing, a man so bruised. Used to soak, you know, but he got over that. Then he ran around. Then he pulled himself up." He leaned across the table as if concluding a shady business dealing. "You women. Stronger than us. Hardier. Take the cold better. Run the marathon better. Live longer. Stand stress better."

He ate his eggs in three large gulps.

"You shouldn't bolt your food," said Misty.

"Do bolt. Always have. Awful for you, but there you are. Right-o. Must jump. Got to wake Gem and get this dog-and-pony show together. See you at the docks. Cheery-bye."

Misty dashed off down the beach. This meeting had lifted her spirits in spite of herself. She ran back to the inn, where she found Vincent wrapped in a blanket, half awake.

"Where were you?" he said. "I woke up in this strange room and you weren't here. I thought my whole life was a dream and that I had never met you. Get over here."

He covered her with blankets and kissed her.

"You've been drinking coffee," he said. "Where did you get coffee? Where's mine?"

"I had coffee with Gem's friend."

"Oh, yeah? While I was asleep?"

"Vincent, he speaks a different language."

"He looks too dumb to speak any language."

"Well, he does. He says 'wizard prang,' 'cheery-bye,' 'lay doggo,' and 'bloody gorgeous.' I've got to write this all down."

"Does this mean I have to listen to this lingo all afternoon?"

"I hope so," said Misty. "You have to listen close and tonight we compare notes."

"Well, cheery-bye," said Vincent. "I'm going to take a shower." He wrapped a towel around his middle and walked off to the bathroom.

The boat held five with a skipper. Someone, it was clear, would have to stay behind.

"I'll stay," said Misty. She felt tears in the back of her eyes, tears of pure self-pity. Wasn't it right that she should stay back and let that happy, homogeneous party float off without her?

"I'll stay with Misty," said Vincent.

"I'll stay," said Guido. "I don't like jigging. I'm a fly-casting man."

"No," said Holly. "I'll stay. I hate fishing. If Misty hates fishing too, we'll stay together."

They stood together on the dock and watched the boat pull out.

"Let's go have breakfast," said Holly. "Then we'll have to go into town. Our room has cooking facilities and I thought if the boys get lucky we'd have a feast."

They walked down the beach toward the inn.

"Is something wrong with you and Vincent?" Holly asked.

Misty had always kept up an elegant defense around Holly. It was necessary that they get along, but not necessary that they be friends. The fondness between them was based on acceptance, Misty felt. Holly had never asked her such a question before.

"I realize that we've never had a really personal conversation," said Holly. "It's just that you looked so stricken at dinner the other night and were so silent in the car and at dinner last night. That isn't like you."

Misty wrapped her coat more firmly around her. There was a lump in her throat. Holly slipped her arm through Misty's. This gesture undid Misty entirely. She stopped walking and began to cry.

"Gracious," said Holly. "You are upset. Sit right down."

They sat down on the cold sand. Holly put her arm around Misty, who continued to weep. Then, abruptly, she stopped.

"I'm all right now," she said.

"You certainly are not all right," said Holly. "What on earth is going on?"

"Nothing," said Misty. "Nothing except self-pity. Just a little spate of it."

They sat on the sand in silence watching the gulls. Then Holly spoke.

"I know something's wrong and I'm sorry you won't talk to me. I've often wished you would talk to me. I always feel you like me out of accommodation to Guido and Vincent's friendship, but that if you had to pick, you wouldn't in fact like me one bit."

"That's not true," said Misty.

"I think it is," said Holly. "For example, the other night at dinner I was in a panic. I was so embarrassed listening to that idiotic cousin of mine go on and on and on. I said to myself: 'Lucky Misty. She has that adorable, smart cousin Stanley. I have a cousin who reflects badly on me.' I thought to myself: 'Well, if Misty ever thought I was useless, she's sure of it now if that's what I'm related to.'"

Misty was startled. She had never heard Holly talk in this way. It rather alarmed her. She was used to the smooth, cool, unflappable Holly.

"And now," Holly continued, "there's clearly something wrong and not a thing I can do to help."

"If I tell you what it is, you'll laugh at me," said Misty.

"Try me," said Holly.

"I was jealous of Gem," said Misty. "Violently jealous. I took one look at her and knew that she was all those girls Vincent ever fell in love with in one package. Sometimes I think Vincent married me only because he thought it would be good for him—that if he wanted to grow up, I was the sort of person he would marry, whereas left to his own devices, someone like Gem would have been his natural choice."

"Isn't this extraordinary?" said Holly. "The things you find out about people you think you know. Jealous of Gem! Dear God, Gem is a smudge on a picture frame. Gem is a public annoyance. Look at the sort of people she runs around with. That John Perkins who speaks British Nautical World War Two slang. Gem isn't worth the leather on her boots. Gem! Gem isn't fit to kiss the hem of your blue jeans."

"It doesn't matter," said Misty. "Well, there you are. You think I don't like you and I'm jealous of the cousin you think isn't fit to kiss my hem."

"And you think that Gem is out there flirting with Vincent?" said Holly.

"Yes."

"And you think Vincent will flirt back?"

"Vincent always flirts. He flirts with Juliana."

"As long as we're talking about this," said Holly, "I'll tell you what I thought the first night I met you. You came to dinner, remember? I was frightened to death of you. This is a girl who can give Vincent a real run for it, I said. I was amazed that he was lucky enough and smart enough to fall in love with you. A few days later I had lunch with him. He probably never told you. Men don't have much emotional memory for that sort of thing. I know he wanted to know what I thought but he was too embarrassed to ask. So I told him."

"What did you say?"

"I said that if he didn't marry you fast he'd be making the mistake of his life. I told him he ought to land you quick before you got away. I said: 'Do you suppose Misty will ever approve of me?' "

"Approve of you?"

"I don't work," said Holly. "I'm lazy. I don't do anything very important. I don't even know how intelligent I am. I just live day to day enjoying myself."

"This makes me feel awful," said Misty. "I was so grateful to you for my wedding breakfast I hardly knew what to say. I'm so mushy that to restrain myself, I never say anything. I'm pigheaded. I never give anyone a chance."

"Now, now," said Holly. "None of this self-criticism. I'm fairly impenetrable after all. At least, that's what Guido tells me. I'm sure it makes a lot of sense that we're the girls they married. They like coolness on the surface. There's nothing like a little propriety to keep people shaking hands is what I say. I'm awfully glad we aren't on that boat. Are you feeling better?"

"Much," said Misty. "Much better. Thank you."

"After I call home to check in on Juliana, let's go into town, have breakfast, and go shopping," said Holly. "Then we can spend a few hours gossiping, or don't you approve?"

"I don't call it gossip," said Misty. "I call it 'emotional speculation.' "

They locked arms and walked down the beach toward the inn.

The boat came back in the early afternoon. Vincent was windblown and ruddy. John Perkins and Gem looked a little green. Guido was carrying a large striped bass.

"Vincent and I caught it," said Guido. "What a struggle. This thing must weigh twelve pounds."

"We've got to go," said Gem. "Take me away, Deering. We're going to a dinner party tonight at the Maynards'."

"Right-o," said John Perkins. He and Gem got into his little red sports car and drove away.

"What a relief," said Vincent. "Not only are they

221

boring, but for a pair of seasoned sailors, they both looked sick and complained all day. Deering or whatever his name is says trawling always makes him dizzy." He took a notebook from his pocket. "See, I do exactly as I'm told. He said 'bloody good show, old man' three times. He said 'heave to, old egg.' He said 'rudder up, my girl.' Let's see, I can't read this. 'Merry hell. Jolly decent. Damned white.' Is that good enough?"

"How awful for you two," said Holly. "Now go clean the fish and then we'll meet in our room after dinner."

Vincent and Misty had a conversation in the shower.

"I was jealous of Gem," said Misty as she soaped Vincent's back.

"I know you were," said Vincent. "I'm glad."

"Glad?"

"I'm always jealous," said Vincent. "I'm always afraid the Talmudic scholar of your dreams is coming to claim you with his fifteen degrees from French universities."

"I don't believe you."

"Well, it's true," said Vincent. "So now you're jealous, although you might have done me the courtesy of picking someone a little more worthy to be jealous of."

"Holly said you would be glad."

"Did you and Holly spend the day talking about us?"

"Yes," said Misty. "It was wonderful."

"This sounds dangerous," said Vincent. "But about your being jealous. How jealous were you?"

"Very."

"Excellent," said Vincent. "Well, I forgive you.

Now you can kiss me and tell me how wonderful I am and how awful you would feel without me."

They kissed under the spray, their soapy arms locked. Misty told Vincent how wonderful he was.

Holly had brought to Salt Harbor a wicker basket filled with four plates, four wineglasses, four place settings of good silver, and linen napkins. The Scott's Fisherman's Inn rented rooms with kitchens for those inclined to eat their catch. In town, Holly and Misty had bought lettuce, potatoes, and a Lady Baltimore cake.

Holly had not forgotten her homemade salad dressing. She had also brought four wooden candlesticks and four beeswax candles as well as a bottle of champagne.

"Perfect," said Holly.

The sea air had given them huge appetites. They polished off dinner, but when the champagne ran out they were suddenly sad.

"Never fear," said Vincent. "There's another bottle. It's in our room. I'll get it." He dashed off and then reappeared with the bottle under his arm.

"I don't remember why I bought it," said Vincent. "Did you tell me to, Misty? You didn't? Holly? Oh, well. Open this thing, Guido. I can't do it without a ginormous explosion."

"Well, here we all are," said Guido as he popped the cork. "Except for Juliana. We always end up sitting around a table drinking champagne."

"I think it's very appropriate," said Vincent.

"What are we going to drink to?" said Holly. "We always end up doing that too."

"To friendship," said Vincent.

They drank to that.

"Now what?" said Guido. "We have to drink to something else."

"Okay," said Misty. "Let's drink to a truly wonderful life."

They raised their glasses and, by the light of the candles, they drank to a truly wonderful life.